Bayou Chase

by

J. D. Webb

This is a work of fiction. Names, characters, places, and incidents are either the product of the author's imagination or are used fictitiously, and any resemblance to actual persons living or dead, business establishments, events, or locales, is entirely coincidental.

Bayou Chase

Cover Art by *Kim Mendoza*

The Wild Rose Press, Inc.
PO Box 708
Adams Basin, NY 14410-0708
Visit us at www.thewildrosepress.com

Publishing History
First Edition, 2023
Trade Paperback ISBN 978-1-5092-4936-7
Digital ISBN 978-1-5092-4937-4

Published in the United States of America

Chase leaned back. "Course I know the name. The bastard killed my wife."

"Mr. Washburn died two days ago."

"Good. Can't say as I'm sorry for the piece of crap. Good riddance. What's that got to do with me?"

"Well, his death is somewhat suspicious."

"You accusing me of doing it?"

She shook her head. "No, just conducting an investigation. We got your service records. Very impressive. Delta Force, two tours in Iraq, sniper school, wounded and discharged."

"Honorable discharge."

"Yes, honorable. You also excelled in house-to-house penetration."

"Look, Detective, I didn't shoot him. I would love to have had the chance to put him in my sights, but I didn't."

"He wasn't shot."

"How'd he die?" He opened his hands palms up.

"He drowned in his bathtub."

"All due respect, Detective, I think we're done here, unless you think I swam up the drainpipe and took him out."

"You understand our concern? You have the skills to pull this off."

"That doesn't equate to guilt, does it?" Chase stood up. "Am I free to go?"

Menendes stood as well. "Yes, as I said we are investigating all possibilities."

"As far as I'm concerned you should have done a better job of investigating my wife's murder. Then we wouldn't be here, would we?"

"Mr. Anderson, I was not involved in that case, and I assure you, if I was, you're right, we would not be here now. Have a good day. An officer will be outside to take you back home."

Acknowledgments

I've been a writer since 2002. Along the way there've been many who have helped me be a better writer, better friend, better husband, and a better person. Fellow authors including my fantastic writing group who drag me into some semblance of cognizance, world class talent like William Kent Krueger, John Gilstrap, David Morell, and Jeffery Deaver, who freely gave of their time and knowledge to a struggling amateur.

My soulmate, and first editor, who I lost in March 2021 was there for 53 fabulous years. I would not have changed anything about those times. I wish I could have had her input for this one. She was my favorite fan.

Also, a shout out to Kayla Vincent, the Public Information Officer for the Calcasieu Parish Sheriff's office. She graciously provided much needed help about the operation and procedures of their office. I appreciate that help as I refuse to make any law enforcement in my books look incompetent or moronic as too often happens in books, movies, or TV. They are too valuable for this society we hang around in.

Without any of them my words would have rattled around locked into my somewhat warped brain.

Then there is my sister, Carolyn, who has steadfastly remained by my side. Her encouragement, listening to my chapters even when she might have wanted to play with her grandkids, and overall being a rock, I rely on. Of the people inhabiting this rock they call earth, given the choice I would still choose you as my Sis. Bubba thanks you.

Prologue

Eighteen months earlier, Naperville, Illinois

There she is. Donnie Washburn followed the beauty he'd seen a week before in that same grocery store. He watched her remove her winter coat and place it into her cart. It was warm inside, and Donnie had already unbuttoned his camouflaged, hooded jacket.

She reminded him of Meg Ryan with short blonde hair twitching as she walked. Same long-legged gait and wearing that soft smile. Her girl-next-door look made his breath catch. Her hips gently swayed under a knee-length light blue skirt, legs toned and smooth.

The skirt accented her curves as she leaned over. He licked his lips. Surely his euphoria had nothing to do with the line of dust he'd snorted that morning. It was love. He had to have her. For sure.

****

Doctor Lily Anderson hummed as she almost floated through the store. She planned a celebratory dinner for the private reveal she would share with her husband, Chase. As she studied the packages of steaks, an icy ripple ran up her spine. She turned. No one was behind her except another shopper in a camouflaged coat. She laughed at herself and dropped two juicy T-bones into the cart with the bottle of champagne, two huge baking potatoes, makings for a salad, and ingredients for a cherry pie.

Lily had decided a feast for Chase would be the perfect way to make the announcement. The visit to her doctor at Northwestern Hospital, the same hospital she practiced reconstructive joint surgery, confirmed the pregnancy. She had no qualms about motherhood. How could she when her mother approached perfection in her eyes? She smiled. Her only concern, even if only a half-hearted concern, was how would Chase react?

Would he relish being a dad? Of course, he would. And he'd be a great dad. Chase was the one she'd always dreamed of marrying. Not the knight-in-shining-armor dream, but a kind, considerate, compassionate man who she knew truly loved her. And in her opinion kind of a hunk, too.

Their relationship had begun when she'd rebuilt his right knee damaged in Afghanistan from an IED explosion. At first, she rejected Chase's requests for a date. He was just trying to show his appreciation for her work. But he was so darned persistent. She had agreed to a one-time dinner and things took off from there.

Lily finished her shopping, pushed the cart out the door, and headed home.

A gray Kia pulled out behind her.

****

Donnie tightened his hands on the wheel as he tried to keep his cousin's Kia Sportage from weaving. That early morning buzz was really working on him. He concentrated on following the happy lady from the store. No imagining it. She'd smiled at him. This wouldn't be the first time he'd connected while grocery shopping.

This time, though, it wasn't a kid from college. This was all woman. He couldn't get her image out of his mind. When he'd spotted her a couple of weeks ago at that store, he'd lost her when he couldn't get to his car quickly enough. She was perfect. And now he was on her trail.

Twenty-minutes later, the Meg Ryan look-alike turned into a cul-de-sac and pulled into a driveway two houses from the entrance. When her garage door raised, she stopped just inside, and then got out. The car's rear hatch lifted, and she removed two bags of groceries, leaving two others, and entered the house through the inner door.

Donnie parked three houses past, tucking his car behind a local plumbing van. He got out and stood beside the driver's door. No one at any of the houses was outside. Perfect. He walked down the sidewalk, took out his cell, and put it to his ear to look like a normal pedestrian in the neighborhood. He approached the open garage and stepped inside. He stopped beside the inner door, took out his knife, and waited.

****

Once the champagne was in the fridge and the perishables were stowed, Lily turned to retrieve the remaining two bags in the car. Her phone's ring tone diverted her to the purse. She dug out the phone and accepted her husband's call. "Hey, Chase, how'd therapy go?" She swiped a hank of unruly hair from her eyes.

"They keep giving me the old no pain, no gain spiel. Seems to be working. Made a hard three miles today." He sounded upbeat.

"Had no doubt that as stubborn as you are you'd do well. I'm proud of you."

"Stubborn? Okay, if I hadn't been stubborn, we'd never have gotten together. I consider it a positive trait."

"Shows how the male mind works."

"Would it be okay to stop and see Randy? Won't stay long but he's had a setback. I'd like to give him some encouragement. "

"What kind of setback?"

"Lung collapsed again. Got him stabilized for now. He took the bullet that was meant for me, and I'm going to do anything I can for him."

"No problem. Understand. Do what you can."

"See you soon. Love ya."

"Back at ya. I'm making dinner and you don't want to miss it."

"No way. Looking forward to it."

****

Donnie heard her end the call and saw the door open. As she descended the two steps, he grabbed her around the throat and pressed his knife along the side of her face.

"Just keep calm. If you scream, I'll cut you. Be a shame to mess up such smooth skin."

"You keep calm as well. I have money and credit cards in my purse. I'll go get them."

"No. I think we'll get them together. Inside."

They shuffled up the stairs and into the kitchen. Her designer purse was resting on the center island. Should be a good bit of cash there. But he wasn't just there for money.

"Where's the bedroom?"

She pointed down the hallway and Donnie relaxed the knife. He shoved her in front of him. As she moved past the kitchen sink, she grabbed a fry pan drying on the counter and whacked him on the knee.

"Ow." Donnie sunk to the floor grabbing his knee.

She came at him again with the pan and got in two

more blows, one to the same knee and the other to the midsection, before he rose and punched her in the jaw. She stopped and sucked in air and shook her head as if to try to clear the stars. But she refused to quit. She grabbed his hair and clawed her fingers across his face.

He swung and connected. She reeled back and her head thudded on the corner of the granite stove top. She collapsed and ceased moving.

Donnie stared for a few seconds. She still didn't move. He felt for a pulse. None. *Oh boy, Dewey and Drew are gonna be pissed.*

He looked down at the woman. *Well, I'm not done yet.* He gently picked her up and carried her into the bedroom.

A half hour later, he dug the wallet out of the purse. He paused a moment when he saw her name. Lily. Fitting. She had been as perfect as that delicate white flower. Without counting it, he stuffed the wad of bills into his pocket, and left through the garage, closing the door using the button on the wall.

Limping to his car, he pulled away from a plumber's van parked next door and floored it. Crash! He didn't see a neighbor lady exit her driveway at exactly the same time. He T-boned her Toyota.

Donnie woke an hour later in handcuffs in the back of a police cruiser.

Then a cop began to question him.

Two hours later Chase Anderson returned home, and his world dissolved.

Chapter 1

Lake Charles, Louisiana, Present day

Chase Anderson sipped the steaming cup of strong, black coffee. The musty smell of decaying wood threatened to overpower the aroma of his favorite blend. The sun had just appeared through the moss-covered trees surrounding his Louisiana cottage as he stood on the small deck in back of his new home. A soft April wind tickled the branches of the trees giving them an almost musical feel. Lazy ripples in the bayou foretold the arrival of one of the ever-present gators feeding near the shore. He wondered if it was old Henry, the 14-footer, who reigned as king of these waters.

Chase relaxed in the Adirondack chair on his porch and finished his coffee. He crossed his legs and watched fish jump in the river, hoping the sun's reflection on the water would soothe him. Was there anything that could sweep away for even a minute the violence and anguish that seemed to constantly swirl through his mind? No, it was something to live with. Hopefully someday the beautiful memories he and Lily had experienced would surface. Someday. Soon, please God.

The idyllic scene before him failed to deflect the anguish over the last year of hibernation. The binge drinking for the first three months, then his awakening to the realization that Lily would have been ashamed of him. He could almost hear her whispering in that soft Cajun accent, "You're not a pig. You're worthwhile and to waste your life when mine's over is shameful. Now, go git yourself cleaned up and live. For me if nuthin' else." He smiled.

Nearly one and a half years ago Lily was taken from him. Much as he tried to avoid it, the memory of the day he discovered her lifeless body, played over and over in his mind. The drinking only made it worse, and he'd stopped cold turkey seven months ago.

Lily, a surgeon who used her limb reconstruction expertise to replace Chase's knee, after it shattered from an IED in Iraq. She guided him through therapy. Gut-wrenching, agonizing pain and frustration even worse than the Delta training he'd endured in the service. Lily, ever patient and gentle, led him to a full recovery. Calling him the bionic man with the metal knee he now possessed.

It took Chase four months just to get Lily to have dinner with him to thank her for all she had done for him. As he hoped, they hit it off immediately. She took him to Louisiana to meet her parents, Beau and Charlene Thibodaux. Beau, short for Beauregard which he hated, was a lawyer semi-retired from a successful practice in Lake Charles. A giant of a man, six foot four with a full head of wavy silver hair never fully combed. His glasses continually rested midway down his nose in the middle of a round red-cheeked face. A small goatee trimmed to a point punctuated a dimpled chin. His roar of a laugh, ear piercing and contagious.

Charlene a registered nurse at the local hospital with a ready smile, captivated everyone she met. Chase's parents had both passed and Charlene demanded Chase call her Mom. And she relished being a mom for the son she'd never had but always dreamed of.

Theirs was a marriage made in heaven, Lily always said. They spoke the same thoughts, sometimes simultaneously. Arguments lasted until one or the other smiled and said, "You win." Didn't matter who won, playful making up invariably culminated their confrontations.

****

Beau had built the fishing shack Chase currently lived in. Calling it a shack was almost a crime. Stilted and situated on a beautiful bayou, the fourteen-hundred-square-foot home had all the comforts. Full kitchen, bedroom upstairs and down, huge TV and entertainment room and fully appointed sports room. Fishing, hunting and boating equipment filled a small shed in back.

This had been Chase's secluded haven to repair himself after his loss. Especially heartbreaking for him and his in-laws the autopsy report revealed Lily had been three months' pregnant. They shared a painful recovery.

But they endured additional heartbreak when they learned additional details about the police investigation. The man responsible for Lily's death had been arrested. DNA evidence confirmed the man's guilt.

Donnie Washburn high on drugs, had followed Lily to their Chicago home when she returned from a mall shopping trip. He forced his way in and brutally raped and murdered her.

But in a mishmash of legal incompetence the police property department mishandled the evidence. It was contaminated and would never be allowed in court. The only charge they could bring was breaking and entering. The man, Donnie Washburn, would serve maybe one to two years, maximum.

Chase had to be physically removed from the police station when he made one of his frequent visits inquiring about his case and found out. They had an officer drive him home and try to calm him down.

Once the policeman left, he roamed his home wrestling with the realization that Lily's killer would eventually be released and could devastate other people's lives. Destroy them like his had been destroyed. His conscience would not let that happen. This person couldn't be allowed to get away with his crime. Chase wouldn't let him.

Chapter 2

August twelfth last year he made up his mind to rectify a wrong and maybe bring closure. What a worthless word. Closure. Who could possibly ever get closure from this? Certainly not him. And he didn't want it. No. Convinced that would never happen Chase decided to see to it, personally, that Donnie Washburn must pay for his crime.

That night, Chase dressed in black jeans, black T-shirt, and black baseball cap with no lettering. Stuffing his Glock .22 in the back of his belt and securing his six-inch hunting knife in his right boot he set out once again to surveil Donnie's apartment house. He'd spent two weeks staking out the residence.

Parking four blocks away he rounded the corner of Donnie's block. Chase consciously hunched over to appear less conspicuous. With a six-foot-two-inch frame easily carrying his two-hundred-fifteen pounds, his normal stature would be noticeable.

Donnie's three-story apartment house in a seedy part of residential Lombard, Illinois, seemed squeezed between two similar narrow buildings. Most windows were dark at just after eleven at night. The unlocked apartment building front door allowed easy entry. Unrecognizable music wafted from at least three apartments as Chase made his way up the narrow stairway.

When he reached the top floor, he stopped, peeked around the corner. Empty hallway. At Donnie's apartment, the second door on the right, he listened for a while and remembered Donnie's smirk at his arraignment. His arrogance and swagger burned into Chase's brain. Scratch marks on the man's face from his wife's struggles still raw and prominent. Donnie, now out on bail pending sentencing, had come home two hours earlier.

At the hearing, Donnie had made several turns to gaze at Chase with that crooked sneer despite admonitions from his lawyer. Donnie just shook his thick, black hair and faced forward. He placed his tattooed arms wide across the pew where he sat next to the attorney. It made Chase's blood boil. Also, it had made his decision that much easier.

From previous nights watching Donnie's place, he knew the man would wait till late to go bar hopping and drug purchasing. Right now, according to previous stake outs, Donnie would be readying for his nightly activities. Chase pulled on a pair of surgical gloves and approached the door. What some call music resonated loudly from the apartment. Chase took one last look down the hall. Still empty. None of the other three rooms on this floor had lights under the doors.

Chase leaned in placing his ear on the door's wood panel. Only music. He drew his knife to undo the inside chain. Once done he tried the doorknob. Beautiful. It was unlocked. He eased the door open and took a quick look inside. Empty.

A threadbare couch sat against the wall. Spots on the upholstery didn't match the design. He slipped in and quietly closed the door. Beer cans, empty pizza boxes and chip bags littered the room. The kitchen sink toward the back was buried in dirty dishes and pans.

Chase eased down the hall. Two closed doors faced the hallway. The one on the right was where the loud music came from. He opened the door a bit, the slight squeak hardly noticeable. Donnie sat in his tub, head lolling on the rim. The chest high water threatened to spill over with any movement. A small table sat next to the tub, containing a boom box and the sparse remnants of a line of drugs on a plate.

Chase leaned over and shut off the music. The silence was immediate. Donnie looked at the table probably trying to figure out why the music stopped. Chase stepped over and showed Donnie the knife.

"Hello, Donnie."

"What the hell you doin' in my bathroom?" Donnie's eyes bugged out. He stared at the knife.

"I wanted to let you see me before I end your miserable existence. You know who I am?" Chase waved the knife in Donnie's face.

"You're the guy. The husband." Donnie's words slurred.

"Yeah. You took my reason to live, now I'm gonna see to it you don't mess with anyone else."

"Can't do that. I'm not guilty. Jury said so." Donnie's head flopped back on the rim.

"What you did to my wife won't go unpunished." Chase grabbed Donnie's hair and pushed him under water. He let him flail around for a few seconds. Water spewed out. Donnie's hands grabbed at Chase's wrist. Finally, he pulled him up.

Spitting and spewing water Donnie drew in a choking breath. "Please." His pleading eyes bugged out.

Chase clenched Donnie's hair tighter and stared into those eyes. "No." He pushed once more, holding him under. Soon the man quit moving. Chase thought he would be satisfied, have a conclusion. It didn't happen.

He took one more look at the man who had caused uncontrollable pain. He turned the music back on, wiped a smudge from the floor where his boot had made an impression, and let himself out of the apartment. He descended the stairs, removed his gloves, and stuffed them into his pocket.

He walked back to his car, climbed in, and eased in a deep breath. On the way home he visited a mall where he threw his gloves into a dumpster. He took a hot shower and went to bed. He had no trouble sleeping.

Two days later the police showed up at his place and took him to the station for questioning in the death of Donnie Washburn.

Chapter 3

Chase sat on one of the three metal chairs in the interrogation room with his hands folded on the tabletop. He checked his watch once more. Twenty-two minutes since they had led him to the room. They told him they had questions, and no arrest warrant had been issued.

He recalled his visit to Donnie. Had he left any trace evidence? Had he made a mistake? Didn't matter. He'd made the creep pay. He felt no remorse.

At the twenty-seven-minute mark the door opened, and a Black woman officer entered. Her nametag identified her as H. Menendes. She sat in the chair opposite him. Chase guessed her to be maybe mid-thirties. About five-foot two, she should have been three or four inches taller based on weight-to-height charts.

"Mr. Anderson, I'm Detective Menendes. Sorry for the wait. I was on the phone and couldn't get off. Did they tell you why you're here?"

"For questioning but I don't know what about."

"Can you account for your whereabouts two days ago around eleven pm?"

"Two days ago? In bed. Usually in bed 10:30 to 11:30. Why? What's going on?"

"Do you know the name Donnie Washburn?"

Chase leaned back. "Course I know the name. The bastard killed my wife."

"Mr. Washburn died two days ago."

"Good. Can't say as I'm sorry for the piece of crap. Good riddance. What's that got to do with me?"

"Well, his death is somewhat suspicious."

"You accusing me of doing it?"

She shook her head. "No, just conducting an investigation. We got your service records. Very impressive. Delta Force, two tours in Iraq, sniper school, wounded and discharged."

"Honorable discharge."

"Yes, honorable. You also excelled in house-to-house penetration."

"Look, Detective, I didn't shoot him. I would love to have had the chance to put him in my sights, but I didn't."

"He wasn't shot."

"How'd he die?" He opened his hands palms up.

"He drowned in his bathtub."

"All due respect, Detective, I think we're done here, unless you think I swam up the drainpipe and took him out."

"You understand our concern? You have the skills to pull this off."

"That doesn't equate to guilt, does it?" Chase stood up. "Am I free to go?"

Menendes stood as well. "Yes, as I said we are investigating all possibilities."

"As far as I'm concerned you should have done a better job of handling the evidence in my wife's murder. Then we wouldn't be here, would we?"

"Mr. Anderson, I was not involved in that case, and I assure you, if I was, you're right, we would not be here now. Have a good day. An officer will be outside to take you back home."

Chapter 4

Chase shook his head to try to wash away the vivid memories. His coffee was cold so he headed for the microwave. He had to figure out where to go from here. Couldn't just mooch off his in-laws forever. Needed to find something to do.

First off where do I want to live? Should it be somewhere close to the Thibodeaux's? Lake Charles or somewhere else? Then what about working? And what job? Not many jobs around for ex-snipers. And who needs a Pashtu translator in Louisiana? They say when out of the service use your learned skills. Hah, I'll just go ask Beau if he knows anyone who needs an assassin.

Okay get serious. But first, warm up your coffee.

While the microwave whirred, Chase's phone buzzed in his pocket. Few people had his number. When he tapped the screen, he recognized the caller ID.

"Detective Menendes, should I say nice to hear from you? What's it been, two weeks since our last talk?"

"Not necessary. In fact, you may be one of the last people I want to talk to. But it's ah, shall we say a courtesy call."

"I'm listening." He took a tentative sip of coffee.

"This is off the record, Mr. Anderson. You know I think your story of non-involvement in Washburn's demise is BS. Also, off the record, I've given it a lot of thought and came to the conclusion, I might have done the same thing in your shoes. Not condoning it, just understanding. You get my drift?"

"Yep."

"Anyway, I want to pass on some information I think you should be aware of."

"Go on."

"Every case we handle has a number and file as you know. Washburn's case is mine and in the last couple of weeks his twin brothers have been in to see me wondering why we aren't looking for Donnie's murderer. I've explained that the case is closed, and death was officially determined to be an accidental drowning. Autopsy showed he was full of drugs and no other signs point to a murder."

"So, they're not convinced?"

"On the contrary. They are adamant that Donnie was killed. But that's not the only problem."

"Okay."

"Don't ask me how, but they knew we interviewed you. I told them they had the wrong name. But somehow, they knew. And the only way they could be sure is if they read it in the file. One thing I know, they did not see the file from me."

"I appreciate the info, Detective. I'm not worried about a couple of bozos coming after me."

"Mr. Anderson, these aren't your average run-of-the-mill bozos. They're mob connected and not stupid. They have smart lawyers because only one of them has ever served time. For assault and battery. That's why I called. If they saw your file, they may be able to find you."

"Well, that makes the pickle more sour, doesn't it?"

"I don't say this often, but I like you. I sympathize

with your situation. And I'm gonna do something that could get me in a bunch of trouble. I have your email address so I'm going to send you a message from my personal account. You receive it and destroy immediately. I'll deny ever sending it. Use it to protect yourself and know who you're up against."

"I'm indebted to you. You will not be compromised by me. I swear."

"I'll hold you to that. I wish you luck and hope you have a chance to find happiness. Don't want to see you in Lombard ever again. Right?"

"No desire to make a visit. Take it to the bank." He hung up. Twenty minutes later a notification alerted him that an email had arrived.

Among the many features of the shack, it included a fully equipped nine-by-twelve-foot office between the bedroom and the bathroom. Beau had used it to prepare briefs, research legal documents and examine law cases. Three of the room's walls were floor-to-ceiling bookcases. The wall to the right contained case law for Louisiana, Texas and Federal. On the left a case with glass-enclosed shelves displayed his prized book collection, ranging from the complete works of Shakespeare, Alexander Dumas, Mark Twain to Louis L'Amour. The smell of old books permeated the room.

A newer MacBook, Beau had given him, sat in the middle of a flat-topped teakwood desk with small pull-out drawers on either side. An eight-foot window over the desk faced the bayou and Chase wondered how the old man got any work done with such a stunning view.

He punched the start button and entered his password. The email from Menendes' personal account, not from the police department, listed two males.

Andrew Washburn, born 11/23/1991, weight 185 lbs., brown hair, height 6 foot 2 inches, race white, eyes hazel, five-inch scar on left arm. Both arms fully tattooed. Charge of aggravated battery of a police officer. Length of sentence 12/18/2014 to 2/7/2016. He had other charges noted but dismissed for known damage to property (compensation paid), possession of cannabis, possession of drug paraphernalia dismissed.

Dewey Washburn, born 11/23/1991, weight 215 lbs., brown hair, height 6 foot 3 inches, race white, eyes brown, no identifying scars, tattooed arms, and neck (with coiled snake.) Numerous charges filed all dismissed for lack of evidence or witnesses. Battery, assault, firearm discharge, protection racketeering, threats of violence.

Menendes had added that both men were rumored to be under investigation by the FBI, but for unspecified crimes.

"You are hard at it I see."

Chase started. "Hey, Beau. Just checking email. Didn't hear you come in. What's up?"

"It's a beautiful day and I was wondering if someone I know might want to join me for some prime fishin'."

Chase looked at his watch. "Still early enough in the morning, I guess. They might be biting at 8:14. Why not?"

Beau smiled and waved his thumb. "Come on let's git."

They grabbed poles and tackle from the shed outside and headed for Beau's boat. A 17-foot bass boat with all the accessories. The short path to the river had been smoothed and embedded with gravel to accommodate Beau's arthritic left knee. The weight he carried didn't help. He had bragged to Chase that he was down to a trim two hundred thirty-seven pounds.

Today though, he seemed to be limping less than usual.

"Your leg feeling better? Not grunting as much."

"Hah. Yeah, yesterday got me a cortisone shot. Gives me three or four days moving better. Doc says I can't put off a replacement any longer. So today let's enjoy."

They reached the boat and Chase steadied it for Beau to climb in. Once he was settled, Chase cranked the motor and they aimed for their favorite spot.

The bright sun had been up only a couple hours, but both men felt its presence. Already the humidity caused Chase to sweat. They glided slowly taking in the scenery. Beau prepared his line and unwrapped one of his Cuban cigars and licked the end.

"Thought you gave those up for good."

He winked. "Gave 'em up for good in the house and around Char. But not out here. I'm too old to have any other vices so I'm stickin' to this one."

Chase grunted. "If Char finds out, you won't have any at all."

"Char doesn't miss anything, Son. She can smell it on me so I can't hide it. She gives me some slack when it comes to cigars. And it's not like I'm out here every day smokin' and drinkin'." He reached into the band of his floppy fishing hat and dug out a pack of matches. Soon cigar smoke puffs drifted in the breeze.

They reached their spot and trolled the water. Beau sat in the captain's chair while Chase stood on the front panel where he could engage the trolling motor if need be. The westerly wind gently bent the grasses and cattails along the bank. It and the smoke helped keep the bugs from being too bothersome.

Chase began to wonder if he'd ever get a bite when he felt a nibble on his line as he brought it back from a cast. He let it sink a bit and gave a tug on the lure once more. A fish attacked the bait and he set the hook. It began to run. Chase let the line go a bit and then began to pull the fish back toward the boat. His rod bent almost in half.

"You got a good one there. Looks like we might have a fish fry tonight with some fresh ones. Bring her in and I'll net it for ya." Beau laid his rod in the boat and lifted the net.

Chase reeled the line and when the fish swirled near the boat, Beau dug the net into the water and landed it next to his pole.

"You got a large mouth five pounder at least. Look at him. He's a beaut'."

"Does look like one to save." Chase clamped the fish scale on and held it up. "Four point nine pounds. He'll taste real good." Chase dropped the bass into the live well and grabbed his pole.

"Why is it that when we go out you always git the first fish? This is my boat."

"I guess they don't like your cigar smoke."

Beau leaned back and laughed. "Maybe so, maybe so. But I'm not quittin'."

They resumed casting and retrieving.

"Chase, I wanted to talk to you while we're out here. Char and I are wondering if you've given any thought to what you're going to do with your life? Don't git me wrong. We're not prying or tryin' to push you into something. We're concerned is all. And ready to help if we can."

Chase reeled in his line and stowed it in the boat. "Funny, I was contemplating the same thing just this morning. I feel guilty having you take care of me without me giving back at all. That needs to end."

"We want to make an offer to you. Just an interim offer while you sort things through. You know Eric my handyman had to leave to take care of his momma. Would you consider taking his place, for a while anyway? We'll pay the same wage we paid him. It'll be good for both of us." He slapped his leg. "With this bum knee I'm pretty useless. We need the help and it will lift a burden from your shoulders."

Chase sat on the lid of the live fish well. He thought over the offer for a few minutes. "You folks have done more than I could ever repay, and I can't thank you enough. I wouldn't feel right taking your money. I won't do that. However, I will take you up on the handyman job."

Beau smiled. "Great. We'll work out the details over supper. Char will be thrilled. And so will I when she puts a couple more fish we catch on our plates. With some of her hush puppies that she's fixin' right now."

An hour later they had six nice fish ready to fix for supper. Beau had the last laugh because his five-point three pounder turned out to be the biggest caught.

Chapter 5

Twins Drew and Dewey Washburn stood outside the back door of Bella Porta restaurant in Cicero, Illinois. Their second visit would result in a collection from the owner. That was a no-doubter. What they didn't know was if there would need to be extra persuasion necessary. The owner would realize the lessor of any evils the twins could dream up, would be a less costly weekly payment.

Their boss, Miguel Desantos, extracted protection money from a wide array of local businesses. The twins handled that part of Miguel's business exclusively.

"Let's go talk to Bennie." Drew opened the door and allowed Dewey to enter first. They walked through the kitchen and into the bar side of the restaurant. At 2:30 a.m. the place had closed to the public a half hour ago.

"Hello, Bennie. How's it going tonight?" Drew checked his watch. "Oops, I mean this morning."

Bennie swirled a dish cloth around inside a recently washed glass. The short man, almost as wide as he was tall, didn't look up from his task. His rumpled graying hair tangled with bushy eyebrows that wiggled as he worked.

"I told you guys; I don't need no protection." Bennie looked up and pointed his finger at Drew. "It would be best if you left."

"Bennie, I'm trying to help you. You're being difficult. Look around this place." Drew swept his hand toward the empty dining room. "This is a really nice place. It's amazing how fast something unexpected can happen. My brother and I plan to come and eat here often. Right, Dewey?"

"Yeah, I love the food. The liquor prices seem a bit steep, but I guess that goes with the atmosphere." He walked to the end of the bar and stepped behind the counter just four or five feet from Bennie. "Take this fine Scotch. Got to run seven or eight bucks a bottle, even wholesale."

He held up the bottle to the light. "Doesn't even look watered down." He let the bottle drop and it smashed onto the floor. "Oh my. It slipped."

They heard a door slam in the back toward the restrooms. A man with dark brown, shoulder-length hair walked down the hall and stopped at the end of the bar. "What's goin' on?" He was at least 6' 6" and when he leaned on the bar his muscles rippled.

"Gentlemen, this is Henry, my protection. He takes care of my problems, so I'd advise you to leave." Bennie smiled at Drew.

"Nice to meet ya, Henry. Do you have insurance?" Drew walked over to Henry and held out his hand.

"Insurance? Sure, I got insurance." He straightened up and looked at Drew's hand but didn't shake it.

"Henry, I see we're going to have a meeting of the minds. You're a big guy and maybe you think you can take us. I'm going to give you the advantage. My brother will not participate. Just you and me. How's that? That okay with you, Drew?"

Drew nodded and poured himself a drink from a bottle he retrieved from the array displayed next to the cash register.

24

"You get the first punch, my man. Go ahead." Dewey stuck his chin out, both of his hands hanging loosely at his side.

Henry stared at him. "You gotta be kiddin' me."

"No. Making it a fair fight. Go on. Hit me. You may not connect."

Henry's hands clenched and unclenched into fists. He looked at Drew and then Dewey. He moved into a right-handed boxer's stance. He flicked out a left jab. It was quick and accurate. But Dewey's snapped his head back and the punch barely grazed Dewey's chin. At the same time Dewey swung his left leg into Henry's unprotected left knee and everyone heard a crack.

Henry went down like a bag of bricks, grabbing his knee and rolling on the floor.

Bennie froze in place. He'd never seen anyone stand up to Henry.

"I believe that proves my point. You won't need to hire another bouncer. We'll take care of that. Part of our money back guarantee. It's Monday morning and someone will be here every Monday to collect our fee. Two thousand dollars. First payment is due…let's say now."

Bennie shook his head and opened the cash register. He counted out the money and handed it to Dewey. "Get out." He bent down to help Henry.

Dewey and Drew left through the kitchen out the back.

Dewey rubbed his chin. "I'd say that went well."

"He had a great jab. I thought he was gonna nail you."

"Game of inches, Bro. Fighting is a game of inches, not baseball."

Chapter 6

After a hot shower, Chase dressed for dinner in his white Chinos, a tan short-sleeved western shirt that had been Lily's favorite, and western boots. He drove the ATV so he wouldn't get his clothes dirty. The dusty half-mile road to the main house was hard-packed dirt and gravel unless it rained. Then it became a quagmire, and the ATV an absolute necessity.

On the short drive Chase thought about Beau's offer. He loved doing odd jobs and everyone told him he was good at it. He'd already noticed a few things around the house that needed spruced up. A month earlier he'd added a heavy metal gate at the entrance to the long drive with a sophisticated electronic opener. If someone tried to override the device, it signaled the home with three loud beeps.

The house had survived the Civil War and undergone several renovations. Listed in the National Historic Register, it was a true southern mansion formerly owned by Henry Watkins Allen, a Brigadier General in the Confederate Army and Governor of Louisiana in 1864. Chase still didn't know how many rooms it had. Beau just answered with "lots" when asked. The same answer given when asked for the square footage. Chase estimated at least eight thousand. He'd never been on the third level. It was closed off for now.

A perfectly aligned row of Hickory trees stood

guard over the circular drive in the front of the house. Top limbs grew together to form a leafy ceiling as you drove down the lane. Chase's limited knowledge of flowers stopped at whether they were beautiful or not. Those that hugged the edges of the drive could be so described.

The tiered portico was held in place by four Roman columns at least sixteen feet high. On the first floor two smaller Palladian windows flanked the front door and two larger, about eight feet wide, Palladian windows were set into the red brick façade. Six normal sized windows lined the second story and two tall chimneys protruded from the roof.

He parked the ATV beside the steps up to the porch. He dismounted and took in the scene. How out of place did that vehicle look?

He passed through the kitchen waving to Char and headed to the dining room through the abnormally wide back hall lined with its many family photos.

Char hurried out of the kitchen toward him and motioned. "Come on, darlin'. We're almost ready to sit. My you look nice."

"Decided my jeans needed washing so I had to dress up a bit."

Char shoved her arm through his and pulled him along. She was dressed in a white pant suit splattered with flowers of many colors. Her blonde hair was pulled into a ponytail. Wide cornflower blue eyes twinkled as she entered the dining room.

"Hi, Chase. Just in time." Beau stood at the credenza pouring a glass of his favorite bourbon. "My stomach's been growlin' at me from the smells comin' in here. Let's eat."

The huge table in the oversized dining room always intimidated Chase. When all leaves were attached it comfortably sat fifteen couples. The uncovered polished maple top mirrored the images of the room. Beau always explained, "If you're lucky enough to have somethin' that beautiful why would you wanna cover it up?"

One end of the table was set for four with white bone china place settings. Two massive chandeliers complete with heavy-duty linked steel chain, hung over the table. The finished white birch planks, each thirty-two inches long, six-inches wide, and four inches deep required four massive hooks to hold the weight. Six globes with sixty-watt bulbs encased inside, provided ample lighting and could be dimmed.

The maple paneling would have made a normal room dark and dreary. Three six-foot tall windows faced west allowing a view of the swamp where the bayou swung around behind the house. Built on a small hill that view spread out for miles on a clear day. The china cabinet, credenza and buffet, topped with homemade breads and jam, were white birch matching the chandelier.

"Lettie, we're ready to eat out here." Beau in his seat at the head of the table, gave Char a wink.

"I'm comin' ya old bullfrog. Keep yer shirt on." Out of the kitchen popped Lettie, Leticia St. Croix, the Thibodeaux's personal assistant. She flipped her coal black hair and glided to the table holding two steaming plates.

A full-blooded Cajun spitfire with skin the shade of coffee heavy with cream, she had been with them for seventeen years and took no guff from Beau. Lettie cooked, cleaned, ran errands, and had helped give Lily a streetwise education to go along with the one she received from school. She was only three years older than Lily, and they had become like sisters. And she'd been adopted as family. No one was more devastated than Lettie when Lily died.

She liked to remind Beau that she actually worked for Char and didn't take no orders from him. It was a purely fun adversarial relationship. Although neither would voice it, they loved and respected each other. Lettie took her meals at the table with everyone else.

Lettie served Char and placed a dish in front of Chase. "Mr. Chase, I fixed your fish Cajun style just the way you like it."

"Lettie how can you outdo yourself with every meal? Each one tops the last. I swear I'll need to do at least three miles after supper."

Lettie slapped his arm. "You keep talking like that and everbody think you actually from Cajun country. That's just the kind a oilin' up we do."

She left and returned with Beau's and her plates and took her seat next to Chase.

Beau cleared his throat and said, "Lettie would you say the grace, please?"

Lettie sighed and bowed her head. "I'd be honored Mr. Beau. Dear Lord, bless this food we're about to receive, bless it to our bodies and please forgive Mr. Beau as he sips his bourbon during our prayer. Amen"

Beaux coughed as he drank and glared at Lettie. Char laughed. "Thank you, Lettie. That was beautiful and spot on, wasn't it, Beau?"

"Sorry, I was thirsty." He was beet red and took another sip.

Silverware clinking the plates provided the only

noise for some time as everyone concentrated on their meals. Finally, Chase put down his fork.

"Lettie I'm stuffed like a gulf lobster. You should have your own restaurant."

"I make only recipes from my mama. I hope you left room for dessert. I made a specialty, *gateau de sirop*."

"My French is not good. What is that?"

"You like it too, Mr. Beau. Cajun syrup cake."

"Now we're talkin'." Beau snapped his fingers.

Chase cleared his throat. "I don't want to ruin such a nice evening, but we need to talk. All of us. You too, Lettie."

"Sounds serious, Chase. Anything wrong?" Beau took his last bite of fish and washed it down with some bourbon.

"There could be. This is now confession time. I'm ashamed of my past. You know my drinking problem. For those three months I was constantly wasted. It wasn't entirely due to Lily's death although I'd say ninety-five percent of it was. I had to deal with some PTSB as well. I told you that her killer died. And as I told you his death was due to drowning in his bathtub.

"What I didn't tell you was that I was the one who did it. I couldn't imagine him freely walking in the same town or even the same planet. His arrogance and distain were too much for me. He was going to get away with Lily's murder. I refused to let that happen."

Char released a loud breath. Beau said nothing. Lettie patted Chase's hand.

"I have to live with what I did but forgive me I'm not sorry. I saw death in the service, I caused death in the service, and war is where death normally happens. It's what I was trained to do. I was a sniper, a damn good one. Each of my kills were done as ordered. I would've been satisfied if that guy had been sent to prison. Those would have been orders - to lock him up.

"But no one gave those orders. Someone had to, in my mind. And I was the only one qualified to do it."

"Whew. I had no idea. I'm sorry you had to go through that. Good Lord." Beau slowly shook his head.

Char took a hanky from her purse and dabbed her eyes "Well, I'm glad you did it. Lily deserved justice and as far as I'm concerned you gave it to her." She got up and came over to Chase and gave him a crushing hug. "Thank you for what you did."

"There are times when we have to do something whether or not we have the right to do it. I think you did good. My Lily was the kindest most loving person I ever knew. That beast didn't deserve to breathe one more time." Lettie wiped her eyes on her apron.

"Chase, I want you to give me a dollar." Beau had his hand out.

"A dollar? Sure, what do you need it for?" Chase dug his billfold out, selected a dollar bill, and handed it over.

"You have just hired me as your lawyer in front of witnesses. Everything you just said is privileged and cannot be used against you. As an officer of the court, I must tell you that murder is never condoned or justified. As a father, I'm proud to have you as my son."

"Okay, confession is over. There's something else you need to be aware of. I got a phone call today from the detective in charge of Donnie Washburn's case. That's the fella I've been talking about. Seems as though his twin brothers suspect me of doing away with Donnie. They've pledged revenge against me, and I'm assuming that would include my family.

"That's one of the reasons I accepted your offer of a job. So, I could be here in case they show up."

"Oh, chances are that's just bluster. Normally that kind of thing doesn't happen." Beau wiped his chin with his napkin.

"This one's different. These are hard cases with mob connections. I believe we all need to be on alert. Char and Lettie, when you go into town, I need to be with you. Please don't go by yourself. You will have a safe room in the back. If anything weird takes place, that's where you go."

Char's eyebrows raised. "I didn't know we had a, what do you call it, a safe room?"

Chase smiled. "Your storm cellar will be outfitted as a safe room in the next couple of days. That's my first project. It'll be stocked with food and water, and it'll be secure. Now that I've ruined your evening, let's have some dessert. What do you say?"

"Sounds like a good plan to me, especially the part about dessert." Beau smiled and picked up his fork.

Chapter 7

Chase and Beau sat on the back veranda after dinner, enjoying the sunset. Char and Lettie busied themselves in the kitchen, filling the dishwasher and compiling a grocery list for a trip into town tomorrow. Beau had extracted a cigar but had not yet fired it up.

"You scared of Char smelling the cigar smoke?"

"Yes and no." Beau smiled and licked the end of the cigar.

Chase frowned and took a sip of his sweet tea. "What the heck does that mean?"

"Yes, because she'd give me a talkin' to if I lit it. No, because she lets me git away with it most times. Ya see, she only wants what's best for me. Cigar smokin' isn't good for my health. We both know it. And we both know how much I love these dang things. So, she gives me grief because she loves me and she lets me smoke occasional', also because she loves me. That's how our marriage has lasted thirty-five glorious years."

"I've seen her in action, and I don't think I'd want one of her talking-to rants."

"Got that right. She may be small in stature but there's power in her that can be substantial."

The bayou was beginning its nightly activity. Two crows circled a magnolia tree cawing at a blue jay that had taken up residence in their territory. Bullfrogs grunted to see who was the baddest. Old Henry, the gator, every so often let out a roar that quieted the whole bayou for a time.

"This has got to be the most peaceful place I've ever experienced."

Beau stretched his leg in an obvious attempt to ease the pain in his knee. "Yep. It is that. One of the most beautiful as well, I think."

"Got my vote."

"Chase, we need to do a couple of things based on our conversation at supper."

"Such as?"

"I think you need to talk to Sheriff Tony. He's a good man and ought to be aware of possible trouble. Do you have any weapons?"

"Yes, I have a handgun, but it's buried in one of the boxes you had packed up and moved down here. Never thought about it till now. Guess you're right, I should get it out. What about gun ownership in Louisiana?"

"We're pretty much wide open. Only restrictions are for concealed carry. You can do it but have to have had a law enforcement training officer certify you. Tony can help you with that. You're officially a resident so state laws apply."

"Good to know."

"Tony Bernardo is a fine officer. He and Lily dated just out of high school. He was heart-broken when she went up to Chicago to go to college. You'll like him, I bet."

"We can see him tomorrow while Char and Lettie are grocery shopping."

"My thoughts exactly. Now, one other piece of business you need to know. Char and I have a joint will. It's been changed and you and Lettie are now equal beneficiaries."

Chase inhaled a quick breath. "That's way too much to digest. It doesn't seem right somehow."

"It's done. Paperwork has been filed. We want this, Chase. We have no other children, and we consider you and Lettie, our family. We've been thinking about making it official for a while."

"I don't know what to say. Thank you seems way insufficient."

Beau slapped him on the shoulder. "If we'd been fortunate enough to have a son, I'd have wanted him to be just like you. Now, I'm about to light this sucker up."

"No, you're not, Beauregard." Char stepped out and marched up to his chair. She jammed her hands on her hips. "Don't even go for those matches in the side of that chair. You think I don't know you stashed 'em?"

"Aw now, Char. Let's not git uncivil, okay? I won't light it."

"Damn right you won't. And I know you smoked a couple while fishing. Come on Lettie, let's join the boys."

Lettie swirled out of the door, her yellow, ruffled dress splaying out as she passed Beau. "I love when she puts you down, Mr. Beau. You crawl like a worm." They both took one of the huge white porch chairs.

"Lettie, I consider it a great honor to be put down, as you say. It means a gorgeous woman is payin' attention to me. Even if she's ticked."

Char laughed. "Why thank you, kind sir."

Beau waved his cigar in the air and made a show of stuffing into his shirt pocket. "It was worth the humiliation, even when she referred to me by my entire repugnant name. So there."

The evening filled with laughter, and good-natured teasing felt so much a part of being a family. Since Lily's death he hadn't been so contented and comfortable. Yet hanging there just on the edge of his mind, apprehension lingered. When something in his life seemed too good to be true, his experience told him it usually was.

Chapter 8

Dewey Washburn smacked his brother Drew in the middle of his chest.

"Umph. Hey what the…?" Drew sat up, threw the covers off, and rubbed the spot. "Whatja go and do that for?"

"We gotta go. Time for retribution."

"Retribution?"

Dewey smiled. "Yeah, got a line on where that Anderson fella might be."

Drew jumped out of bed. "Really? Where?"

"Louisiana. Our contact just texted me where that guy's in-laws live. Lake Charles, Louisiana."

"Never been to Louisiana. How we gonna get to leave? You know Miguel is wanting us here for the next drop and our collections."

"Course, but that won't be for at least a week. We can boogie on down there, do our thing, and be back in plenty of time. No sweat."

"I don't know. Miguel made it clear he wants us available 24/7."

"Hey, don't we deserve a vacation? Can't see him denying us that as hard as we been working for him. 'Sides, that commitment we got from the bar man at Raising Spirits will make him real happy."

"Miguel didn't think we could do it, but we did. Two thousand a week to keep anything bad from happening to his bar."

"Get dressed and let's go. We gotta convince Miguel to let us relax on our vacation."

The two brothers packed bags for their trip and left to try to persuade the number four crime boss in the Chicago suburbs to let them go.

****

Miguel Desantos slammed the cell phone down on his table so hard it bounced onto the floor. "Now what we gonna do?" He shook his head, his long black hair with an enhanced silver lock on the right side, windmilled. He ran his hand through it, failing to make it any better.

"What's the matter, boss?" Shonte Williams, a six-foot seven-inch, thin Black man, stopped wiping down a recently refurbished Lexus.

"That was the man. They got a homicide last night. It was Ziggy."

"Ziggy's dead?"

"Seems as though his ol' lady found out he was fraternizing, that was what the cop said, fraternizing, with some other bimbo and she shot him. Good thing he died because where she shot him, his fraternizing days was over anyway."

"Ouch. So, who's gonna do the next run?"

"Don't know. Got to find somebody. Crap!"

As if an answer to an unsaid prayer, Dewey and Drew Washburn entered the converted warehouse. Nine autos in various states of dismembering, or reconditioning as Miguel called it, sat under twelve eight-foot fluorescent lights. Two mechanics worked on the first floor.

Drew never missed locating the two armed, guards

pacing the open upper floor that wrapped around three sides of the building. Both carried Ak-47s.

They walked up to the office, making heavy footfalls on the wooden stairs. Drew handed a brown envelope to Miguel. "Here ya go, boss. The guy at Raising Spirits is on board. Two thousand a week just like you wanted."

"Good work, homies. Good job." Miguel handed the envelope to Shonte. "Put this in the safe."

The man took the envelope and turned to go.

"What a minute? Let's count it to make sure, ok?"

"It's all there. We'd never cheat you, Miguel." Sweat broke out on Drew's forehead.

Miguel patted Drew's shoulder. "I know you wouldn't. That'd be stupid. But I like to be sure."

Shonte counted the money and nodded. "All there."

Dewey sighed. "Miguel, you mind if I ask a favor?"

"A favor. You ask me for a favor?"

"Well, yeah. Me and Drew been working hard. You know that. We'd kinda like to take a vacation. Just maybe a week or so. What do ya say?"

"So, you want a vacation? What is this some kind of company where you get benefits?"

"No, no, nothing like that. Just some time off, that's all."

"Somebody shoot these two." Shonte pulled a Glock and aimed it at Dewey.

Drew sank to his knees. "Oh, God."

Miguel stared for a full half minute and then laughed. He doubled over. "Oh, I got you guys. Drew, I didn't think you could get any whiter, but you just did. Put it away, Shonte. I'm funnin'. Dewey, just pullin' your leg, dude."

"Well, you sure got us there, boss. Had us goin'."

"Actually, I'm gonna give you a vacation. A paid vacation. But there's a catch. One week from today a truck will be parked at the Memphis dock. You two are gonna pick it up for me. Take the money. Shonte give 'em back the envelope. This is your expense money.

"I don't need to tell you that this is the most important job I ever give you. I expect that vehicle to be right here," he jabbed his finger toward the floor, "the same day it's picked up. Got that?"

"No problem. And we appreciate this opportunity, don't we Drew?"

Drew nodded his head so hard his neck cracked.

"Consider it a life and death vacation. Cause if that truck don't get here, you will be shot. *Comprende?*" Miguel pointed his finger at Dewey and tapped it with his thumb. "Bang."

He handed Drew a piece of paper. "Do not fail me."

On their way back to pick up their luggage, the brothers said little. They'd been given the address where the truck would be, a burner phone with Miguel's private number, and the two-thousand dollar's protection money. Dewey mapped out a plan for a trip to Lake Charles and a return through Memphis, while Drew thought about how close he came to being shot.

Chapter 9

After dropping Char and Lettie off at the Super Store in Sulphur, Beau and Chase headed to Lake Charles to talk to Sheriff Tony Bernardo. Beau had called and asked for a meeting. Tony agreed and said to come on in, his morning was clear till 11:00.

Beau owned two cars and loved driving each of them. His favorite, a Silver 1999 Mercury Grand Marquis had been chosen for the trip for the comfort of the ladies. Chase had to admit the car was quite comfortable.

"This old beauty still hugs the road, Chase."

"That it does. How many miles you got on it now?"

Beau glanced at the gauge. "Just over 35,000."

Chase laughed. "So, you put about 1500 miles a year on it? That's all?"

"When Char wants to go for a ride this is what she likes. It isn't often she wants to go. Now ask me how many miles I got on my Hummer."

"Okay I'll bite, how many?"

"I don't know." He laughed. "It's a 2005 that I don't drive too much. I use the Hummer for gettin' around when the roads aren't good, which is almost anytime it rains. One of your jobs will be to smooth out the ruts I make when the dirt path transforms into quicksand. In the rainy season that'll be almost every day.

"Lettie usually drives Char into town or wherever

she wants to go. She hates to drive because she gets upset with the other drivers. She's been hit four times and I think only two of them weren't her fault. Don't tell her I said that. After the last collision she said no more."

"How far's the sheriff's office?"

"Only twelve miles from the Super Store. Just off I-10. 'Bout twenty minutes if traffic is normal."

As Beau had said, they pulled into the parking lot in front of a long flat brick-faced building, in twenty minutes.

Chase chuckled. "Real convenient to have a bail bondsman's office across the street from the Sheriff."

"Those guys don't miss a trick."

The bumper of Beau's Mercury tapped the visitor parking sign as he swung into an empty slot. It shuddered but remained standing. "Never allow enough room for a substantial car to fit in here," Beau growled.

Chase made no comment. He knew Lettie would've made one, though.

When they entered, the reception area was vacant, so they waited at the desk. Three minutes later a uniformed deputy appeared. Chase estimated his age at probably mid-twenties, tall maybe six-foot-two, with a nametag showing T. Johnson. His wavy red hair was shaved down on the sides.

"Mornin' Mr. Thibodeaux. Sheriff's expecting you. Go right on back."

"Thanks, Tim."

The corridor they walked down had, as near as Chase could tell, ten or so occupied desks. Some hidden by pillars.

Beau continued his commentary on the sheriff.

"Tony has over a thousand deputies if you include part-timers. A good detail person. Decent job of cleaning out undesirables. Former marine. Been overseas, two tours when he was younger."

The sheriff stood outside his office. Officer Johnson had obviously announced their arrival.

Beau grabbed Tony's hand. "Good of you to see us, Tony. Say hello to my son, Chase."

"Chase, glad I finally got to meet you. All this old goat talks about is you. Well, and that adorable Charlene. He married way above his class." He playfully poked Beau in the stomach. "Come on in. Can I get you something to drink?"

Beau waved his hand. "No need, Tony. Just finished a huge breakfast. We won't take much time. Besides we let Char and Lettie loose in Walmart. I gotta git back and rein them in before I'm sent to the poor farm."

"I doubt that'll happen, Beau."

In the next ten minutes they filled Tony in on the circumstances of Lily's death and the resulting threat by the twin brothers, minus the part about Chase's involvement.

"Very odd that they know the police talked to you, Chase. They'd have to have access to paperwork to get that information. That department may have a mole."

Chase grunted. "Lots of things to be wary of in that place. With this threat I want to be prepared. I have a weapon and I was wondering if you could suggest a reputable outfit for me to practice. Been a while since I fired anything more than a charcoal pit."

Tony smiled. "I'll get you hooked up with our trainer. Les Atwood. He'll get you up to snuff in no time. Are you wanting a concealed carry permit?"

Chase nodded. "I think it would be prudent."

Beau flexed his leg. "We don't need one on our property, do we? Law hasn't changed on that I think."

Tony waved his hand. "Nope. Castle laws allow use on imminent threat."

"Good."

"Chase, I wanted to express my sympathy on the death of your wife. Lily always had a special place in my heart. I was devastated when I heard the news."

"Thank you. I'm just now climbing out of the deep dark hole I was in."

"If there's anything else I can do for you guys, let me know."

Beau tapped his finger on Tony's desk. "Maybe you could have a patrol roll by every so often. We don't know how credible this threat is but no sense ignoring it either."

"I think we can do that. I'll get the duty officer right on it."

Beau stood and offered his hand to Tony. "I truly appreciate that."

Chase also shook Tony's hand. "Thanks, Sheriff."

"It's Tony. Good meeting you. Don't worry we'll be aware. Give Les Atwood a call about getting concealed carry. He'll be waiting for you to get started."

"Will do."

Chapter 10

Dewey drummed his fingers on the Charger's steering wheel. "Come on Drew. Let's get goin'."

Five minutes later Drew jumped down the stairs and jogged to the trunk of the 2020 Deep Water Blue Pearl muscle car, as he liked to think of it. He stowed his bags inside and climbed into the passenger seat.

"What the hell took you so long?"

"Mrs. Livermore was writing down instructions about Ditka. His favorite dog food, toys, when he needs to go out. Stuff like that."

"That mutt causes more trouble. I'm always waitin' on you because of the stupid dog."

"Hey, he's a full-blooded German Shepherd. Got papers an' everything. I could show him if I wanted. If nobody checked to see where I got him."

"Well, he sure ain't no watch dog. Somebody gives us grief the only way that cur would help is by drowning them in slobber. Let's get outta here."

The engine rumbled to life, and they rolled toward I-355 Veteran's Memorial to head south.

"You bring your gun?"

"Yeah, and ammo. Stashed in the bottom of my suitcase. Before you ask, I got cleaning stuff for it, too. I already broke it down and stashed it in the compartment under the seat. Any more questions?"

"Nope, that ought to do it. I figured we'd head

through Memphis, locate the dock, and scope out where we pick up the truck on the way back. Should be a piece of cake. Easy money, Bro, easy money."

"We should stop there overnight and take in some night life. After all, we got expense money."

Dewey grinned. "We do, don't we? Party time!" He held up his hand for a high five.

Chapter 11

Beau chuckled. "Let's have some fun, Listen to this."

He put the phone on speaker, hit a speed dial, and stuck it in the cup holder, while steering with his left hand.

When Char answered, he asked, "Have you spent all our money yet?"

"I'm trying extra hard, darlin'. Hope the trunk's big enough."

"You keep goin' and I might have to recruit some gang riff raff to add to my client list to drum up more business."

"Go ahead, I'll be sure and visit your jail cell at least once a month." Lettie giggled in the background.

"You hurt me with that one. Where do we pick up a couple of beautiful women?"

"That's your problem, old man, but if you want to get Lettie and me, we'll be at the Walmart grocery door in about ten minutes or so. Whenever we're done."

"See ya then."

****

As Beau suspected, a ten-minute estimate proved woefully inadequate. They sat parked under the shade of a tall oak tree, providing relief from the sun's rays with the door to the grocery side in full view.

"Whenever a woman gives you a time when she'll

be ready and adds 'or so' you might as well settle down with your favorite beverage."

"I hear that, although Lily was very punctual. I was lucky in more ways than I can express." Chase swallowed to ease a sudden tightness in his throat.

"When she was a child, she became captivated by the clock. It was a challenge for her to find out how such a small gadget could tell us the time."

"It was easy to get her a birthday or Christmas present. She had four watches and several wall clocks. Now I know why." Chase smiled.

"Chase, I'm really proud of the way you've recovered from your, ah, shall we say dark period. Char and I worried that you were so deep in despair you'd never git back. "

"I had times where I didn't want to come back. Kept seeing Lily urging me to live. Might sound foolish, but she seemed to be right there. Then I'd try to grab her for a hug and she'd disappear. That would put me back in the bottle again. I seemed to be in the middle of a tornado."

"Well, you persevered, and we were thrilled when you became Chase again."

He patted Beau on the shoulder. "Couldn't have done it without my family. When I lost my parents, that's what pushed me to join the military. I thought I'd never again get any feeling of belonging. I felt it with Lily but still something was missing. To me family is more than one person even as much as I loved her."

"Something else needs to be put on the table, so to speak. Char and I knew that Lily was pregnant."

"You knew? Wow, I avoided talking about it because I didn't want to cause you any additional grief.

She must have called."

"About two days before Lily was killed, Char got a call. She was so happy. She'd never even thought about motherhood. She was planning to tell you the day she was killed. Being a doctor was her life till she met you. Char and I haven't mentioned it because we didn't want to upset you. I'm glad it's out in the open."

"Oh, me too. No secrets from each other, okay? From now on."

"Absolutely."

Beau's cell buzzed. "Hello. Okay we're right outside looking at the door." He hung up. "They're on the way. At least that's what she said."

Char and Lettie pushed a full grocery cart out the door and looked around. Lettie spotted the car and waved.

Beau started the car and pulled up behind a pickup loading bags in the cab. When the truck pulled away, he stopped next to Char and punched the trunk release. Chase jumped out and helped stow the bundles, then opened the door for Lettie while Beau did the same for Char. Men in front, ladies in back. Then they headed home.

"Whew, shopping's gittin' harder and harder." Char's hanky dabbed sweat from her forehead.

"Did you have fun?" Beau grinned.

"I'm beginnin' to hate going there. The crowds. And the outfits women wear. Outrageous. Like they jumped outta the bedroom and came in their jammies. I wouldn't be caught dead in some of stuff they must believe is perfectly okay."

"Times are changin', that's for sure."

"Well, not for the better far as I'm concerned.

Anyway, we're gonna have a great dinner tonight. We got the fixins."

"I guess it was worth the wait of twenty-two minutes instead of ten, or so."

"Beau, it would a been but Mrs. Kerns stopped and I couldn't get her to let me go. Finally told her my ice cream was gonna melt."

"Yep, you always seem to find a body to talk to."

"Well, I can't be rude."

"Honey, you don't have a rude bone in your skeleton, 'cept when you're cussin' me out."

"And when I do, you know you deserve it."

Chapter 12

"Hey, Drew, you don't look so happy. Come on, drink up."

They sat in a crowded Memphis bar, the third one hopped so far, with a band so loud their drinks sometimes jumped on the rickety table.

"I'm not thirsty right now. Think I'm getting' wasted," Drew yelled.

Dewey frowned. "You wanna go?"

"Not just yet. Truth is I miss my little brother. Donnie used to love this."

"Yeah, he sure did. I remember when he turned eighteen. He wanted a beer. By then we were of age, and we got him a six pack. When he tried to chug the first one, he couldn't swallow it."

"Came out his nose. That was classic. We never let him live that down. Boy he learned quick though. He could out drink us both." Drew held up his bottle. "Here's to Donnie."

Dewey clinked his bottle to Drew's and downed the rest of his beer, then slammed the bottle on the table. "You're right. Don't seem as fun as usual. Let's go. We can get an early start tomorrow. The quicker we get to Louisiana, the quicker we can let Donnie rest in peace. I'm feeling ready to do some damage."

"Ok. I'm done."

They stood and pushed through the swaying bodies.

Once outside they turned toward their hotel. They'd picked bars close to their motel so they could walk back. That eliminated the risk of a DUI.

They rounded a corner two blocks short of their destination. Two bearded Black men dressed in black stood about twenty paces in front of them. The street had been deserted till now. One man lounged against the side of a closed business. He wore a short leather jacket, jeans and work boots. A beret sat back on his head. The other man was taller, maybe six-three, with a baseball cap turned backward, a sleeveless t-shirt allowing full view of rippling muscles, jeans, and black sneakers.

The shorter man pushed away from the building. "Say, gents, where you off to?"

Dewey glanced at Drew and nodded. "We're headed home."

Drew turned and looked behind him. "Dewey, got two more guys to the rear."

"Just give some cash and we'll let you pass. Whatever you got will be just enough." The shorter man turned his palms up.

Drew moved so he and Dewey were back-to-back.

Dewey spit on the sidewalk. "We only got a few bucks on us. But you're not going to take 'em. You need to let us be." He pulled out his leather sap and took a few steps toward the tall man.

Drew backed up with him, still facing the two behind. Both were stocky, just under six feet. One looked Hispanic, the other white.

Dewey slapped his hand with the lead filled weapon. "Still time before your appointment."

The tall man laughed. "I got no appointment."

"You will if you don't let us pass. Some ER doctor

is waitin' on you."

The shorter man didn't move. The tall one stepped in and threw a wide punch with all his momentum driving forward. Dewey easily sidestepped and whipped the sap under the man's arm. He could feel at least one rib collapse. The man grunted and fell to the sidewalk.

Dewey turned to the second man and swung a vicious leg kick to his face. Blood squirted from the man's nose, and he threw up both hands to quell the flow. His beret flew off and landed in the gutter.

Drew had punched the closest man to him in the throat. The man was gagging trying to force air into his lungs. The last man hesitated, then turned and ran down the street.

Dewey stood over the first two ready for another blow if needed. "You okay, Drew?"

"I'm fine. I only got to hit one of 'em. You scared the piss out of the last one. He hightailed it."

"Since they wanted our money, I think since we won the fight, we get their money. See what your guy has."

They searched all three. Wallets, cell phones and cash yielded a nice return.

"It's only fair that we divide up our reward, Drew, cause your other guy turned chicken."

He slapped the short man on the head. "You, I'm leaving you your cell so you can call for help for that guy." He pointed with the man's cell and threw it to him. He was still trying to stop the bleeding from his nose. The cell hit his arms and clattered to the pavement.

The first attacker lay rolled into a fetal position; agony etched on his face.

Drew leaned down and yelled at the guy. "you say hi to that doctor for me. Oh my, I hate to see anyone hurting." A tap by the sap on the man's bald head knocked him out.

The two brothers left and made it back safely to their hotel. In Drew's room they took stock of their haul. Over eight hundred in cash, two cells, one a new iPhone that Drew had used his attacker's fingerprint to unlock, and sixteen credit cards.

"Not a bad night's work, I'd say." Dewey handed Drew his share.

"Felt good. I needed to let off some steam."

Chapter 13

The next day, before his appointment with Les Atwood at the shooting range, Chase decided to tackle setting up the safe room as he'd promised. Beau left to go to his office in town and Lettie and Char decided early spring cleaning needed to happen.

He began by listing supplies needed to make the room livable. He'd add things as he thought of them. They'd argued about the cost of the room. Chase insisted it was entirely his expense. With his disability allowance, Army pension, and Lily's life insurance, he had more than enough to live comfortably. This would be a way he could give back to his family.

Chase had discovered the storm cellar on one of his daily walks. To keep fit, in addition to using the exercise room in the shack, he walked at least three miles a day. His knee was almost fully functional. Sideways movement was still awkward, but he could live with that. The pain hardly noticeable compared to when he first began his exercise program three months after his arrival in August, eight months ago. Those first months were spent in deep depression and self-pity. He wanted to forget those days. He'd become a different person. One he was ashamed of.

Chase walked to the house swinging his toolbox, enjoying the breeze. He carried a bucket of soapy water in his left hand and under his arm some cleaning rags

Lettie had scrounged up for him.

Clouds dotted the sky looking dark enough to suggest rain. He felt good. Maybe life was turning around for him. Not that it owed him anything. Often harsh and unforgiving described his life so far. God knows he'd experienced so much of it. But he found joy in this place. He remembered how fondly Lily spoke of her home. He believed he was meant to be here.

Birds chirped, the wind rustled the moss and branches of the willows, and the ever-present bayou noises - gators, insects, frogs - all had become natural and familiar. Even though dangers existed, peace could also be detected.

The house built on a hill allowed drainage to run away naturally. He climbed the drive and approached the back of the house and the shelter. A heavy, gray wooden door, once a lid to a ship's cargo hold, creaked and moaned when he pulled on it. He sprayed WD40 onto the hinges and swung the door until it moved easily. The handle was loose but held. The door opened on a slant of almost forty-five degrees. He descended the three steps into the room.

He'd peeked into the shelter once before but had never checked it out thoroughly. The original owner, an owner of a shipping company and a successful importer and exporter, had dug the shelter under the mansion for safety from hurricanes. The walls, floor and ceiling were salvaged ship decking. The room measured nine by twelve with a ceiling of seven feet. The man had six children and that room had saved their lives through five major storms. Chase had read the history in the owner's logbook discovered in the library.

He turned on a lantern he'd brought. Unexpectedly,

the room seemed only slightly musty. A faint hint of spruce gave off a pleasant odor and, he detected a whiff of linseed oil, that had probably once been used to polish the wood to a gleaming shine. Chase removed cobwebs and tested a chair resting in the corner. It didn't seem too steady, so he pitched it outside and added chairs to his supply list.

Behind the chair was a small, three-shelf storage case built into the wall. The shelves were still sturdy, and he cleaned them as well. Great place to store supplies.

He spent another hour scrubbing down the front and side walls, cleaning the floors and ceiling. He climbed the stairs and pulled the door closed. The thick wood sealed the room and would be difficult to breach. He tightened the door handle. Chase wondered how much air would be available to breathe. Something to determine later. If the owner had seven people in the enclosed room, they'd use up all available air in minutes. The log hadn't offered any clue regarding this.

He continued cleaning the rear wall. Near the top he spotted a small panel with a strap hanging in front. He hadn't noticed the strap before because it hung squarely in front of a seam in the wall. He gave the strap a tug and it disintegrated in his hand. It had been attached to a metal strip so he pulled on it to try to open the panel. It was stuck.

He dug in his toolbox and found his pliers. When he finally managed to pull it open, a stream of stale air hit his face. Shinning his flashlight into the opening, he could see a shaft extending as far as the light penetrated. The shaft, lined with metal tubing, provided air flow from somewhere. So much for that mystery. At least no one would suffocate.

The last wall cleaned; Chase packed up his toolbox. Satisfied, he examined the room. Not a bad place for a hideaway. One item needed to be added to the supply list. Bug spray to eliminate spiders. Char would not set one foot in there if a spider made an appearance. They all recognized her scream when one dared invade her space.

Now to take some target practice, and then pick up the long list of items to furnish the safe room.

Chapter 14

Flashing lights brought Drew out of his reverie. He'd been sleeping while Dewey drove. "You dumb shit. How fast are you goin?" He quickly sat up.

"I got the cruise on. It's set at seventy-three. No way I'm speeding."

"Then why we got a cop behind us, flashing his lights and got his siren screamin'?"

"Don't know. Chill out. We haven't done nothin'."

"What if he checks our trunk, Einstein? I got some weed in there. Crap."

"Just relax, Drew. Can't be anything major. Maybe we got a light out or somethin'."

They slowed and pulled to the side of the road.

Drew started biting his nails. "Where are we anyway?"

"South of Little Rock. Map shows we're near Benton."

Drew turned and peered over the front seat. He spit out a piece of nail. "He's just sittin' there."

"He's runnin' the plates. Checkin' to see if there's any alerts on us. Don't worry, there aren't any. Listen, we're just heading to Texas, just passin' through. Stick to that and we'll be fine. And turn around. Don't look nervous. Cops can tell. Relax. Take a deep breath."

They sat there for a couple more minutes. Then the officer opened his door and stepped out. He rested his right hand on the handle of his weapon and approached the car.

Dewey rolled down his window. "Mornin', officer. What's the problem?"

The cop bent down and looked across at Drew. He was stocky and a mop of curly, brown hair escaped his trooper hat. Dewey guessed his age in his mid-thirties.

"Mornin', boys. You mind puttin' your hands on the dashboard? Just rest 'em there please. Where you headed?"

"We're goin' to Texas, Abilene. Our mom's in the hospital. I didn't think I was speeding. I'm Dewey and this is my brother Drew." Dewey placed his hands around the steering wheel on the dash.

"Can I see your license and registration, please?" The officer placed his left hand on the driver door where the window had rolled down.

Drew fidgeted around in the glove compartment and handed Dewey the documents. His hands shook.

Dewey hoped the cop wouldn't notice. He handed the papers through the window.

"Robbery in Little Rock 'bout two hours ago." He handed the papers back to Drew. "The two guys who did it escaped in a fast, blue car. Your vehicle kinda fits the description."

"You're right this is a fast car but last thing I want is to pay a speeding ticket."

"I don't think there's any need to keep you any longer. The robbers were two Black dudes. When I first saw you with your beards, I couldn't tell if you were black or not. If you assure me, you don't have any contraband in your trunk, I'll be on my way."

Dewey winked at the cop. "If you don't count the

sixteen dwarf illegals we got stuffed in there, we're good." Dewey heard Drew's loud gulp.

The officer stared and then laughed. "Oh, that's a good one. They'll get a kick out of that when I clock out tonight. Y'all have a good day."

They watched the officer, shaking his head, as he walked back to his cruiser.

"I almost had a heart attack when you said that, Dewey. You scare me sometimes."

"Come on. They like a good laugh just like us. Let's get outta here."

Chapter 15

Beau had given Chase a set of keys to both the Mercury and the Hummer. "Take 'em for a drive whenever you want," Beau had exclaimed. "Long as I'm not usin' one."

Since Beau had taken the Mercury to his office, Chase was left with the Hummer to make his appointment with Les Atwood of the Sheriff's office. He'd stowed his well-oiled and cleaned 1911 Springfield EMP in the back. His proficiency with rifles was almost legendary in the Army. With a handgun not so much. He wasn't bad, but his desire for accuracy demanded more practice.

He appreciated that the past three days had been dry. Rain was forecast later in the week, so he wanted to get the big truck back into its stall before that. Cleaning bayou mud and gunk from a Hummer nestled way low on his list of fun activities.

Bayou humidity, which he'd been told lasted six to seven months, had begun in earnest this April morning. The headband of his old Army baseball cap just five minutes into his drive already soaked in sweat. With the light traffic he made good time to the shooting range.

He parked next to a pickup truck, a relic from the eighties. It had seen rugged use, but the bed sparkled. The man in the cab puffed on a thin black cigar, slowly expelling a thick cloud of smoke. When Chase climbed down and retrieved his canvas bag, the man swung out of his truck.

Chase headed for the entrance to the range.

"Howdy?" The man dropped his cigar and stamped it with the toe of his scuffed western boot.

"Hello. Great day."

"Tis that. Tis that. You might be Chase Anderson, right?" The man walked toward Chase with his hand extended. He looked to be maybe mid-fifties and walked with a slight limp.

"Yep. I guess you must be Les."

"Was when I got outta bed this mornin'. Pleased to meet ya." He shaded sky-blue eyes from the sun with his other hand. A beat-up cowboy hat sat back on his head. He was a couple inches taller than Chase's six-two but thinner.

A dark brown western shirt with two button-down pockets was mostly tucked into faded denims. An easy smile revealed four crease lines around his mouth on each side.

Chase accepted his hand and grinned. "I bet the Hummer gave me away."

"You got the makin's of a deputy." He chuckled and slapped the car. "This's the only Hummer within five hunderd miles."

"Let me show you how good I am. You're not a native Louisianan, are ya?" Chase smiled.

Les pointed a finger at Chase. "Amazin' just amazin'. Guilty as charged. From San Angelo, Texas. Was totally beguiled by a little filly from here and she made me relocate. 'Bout thirty-two years ago. Never regretted that decision once. Come on inside, let's see how bad you are."

They entered the long, low one-story building beneath a sign identifying it as the Calcasieu Parish Sheriff's Department Shooting Range. Once Chase's eyes adjusted to the dark interior, he followed Les to a counter. Twelve targets hung on the wall behind with dates and names scrawled across the bottom of each. All had a single hole in the center, no larger than a half dollar. Four of them had been autographed by Les Atwood.

Three men stood around a coffee pot on a table to the left, and one man behind the counter waved at Les. His belly protruded at least six inches over his belt, barely covered by a white dress shirt. Chase would wager the man weighed north of three hundred pounds. His round face defined by ruddy cheeks, two huge black eyebrows, had matching long coal-black, unruly hair.

"Gents, this here is Chase Anderson. He's Beau's son-in-law and will be visiting here from now on." Les shook his finger at the man behind the counter. "Paul, none of that first-time rookie shenanigans is gonna take place. Hear me?"

Paul opened huge hands face up. "Now I told you I don't pull those tricks. That's these other guys." He motioned toward the men at the coffee pot.

"Don't care. Goes for all. Get him signed in. We're gonna do some shootin'."

Chase filled out a registration form, picked up his bag and he and Les filed through a door to the right of the counter into a huge locker room. Les walked over to a line of lockers and twirled a combination lock.

"This is my locker. We can get you one set up if you like. I keep some of my spare practice weapons here."

Inside were at least a dozen handguns in marked

boxes, Glocks, Rugers, and Colts. Les dug in the bottom of the locker and pulled out a metal case the size of a pizza box with a thickness of nine or ten inches.

"Spare?" Chase asked.

"Hah. My wife wants to know what the word enough means to me. Haven't come up with a satisfactory answer yet."

He opened the lid and pulled out a silver revolver and leather gun belt, placing them on one of the benches in front of the lockers. He put the case back in the locker and closed the door.

"This is my show gun." Les wrapped the belt around his waist and picked up the handgun. He flipped open the chamber and checked the inside. "One thing to begin. Even if I know my gun isn't loaded, I always check anyway." He rolled the gun over and the chamber clicked into place. "Let's get to it."

Les led him out the rear door to a large courtyard. The first thing Chase saw was ten life size targets hanging on lines against the far wall. Four men and two women stationed off to the right practiced firing and acknowledged Les.

Les motioned for Chase to stand in front of target two. "Let me see your weapon, Chase."

Chase opened the bag he carried and pulled out his EMP.

"Recently cleaned, I see." Les checked the chamber and worked the trigger. "Got ammo?"

"Sure." Chase handed him a box of 9 mm bullets.

"If you want to stop someone with one shot, I think this'll do the trick."

"Got it. Beau had some of these handy. He has more."

"Don't doubt that, no sir. Beau can shoot. Been out here some." Les pointed to a pair of headsets hanging on a wood panel next to Chase. "There's your ear protection. Load up and take a shooting position. I know you've handled weapons before, but I always start out with basics."

Chase donned the head gear, loaded his gun and took a stance at the start position.

"Okay, that's good, bend the knees a bit. Facing the target is good and accepted practice, Start with that. But if you're in a shootout you should always shoot with your body completely sideways. Ought to practice that way as well. Less of a target. When you're ready, fire. I'll watch." Les donned the second pair of head gear.

Chase remembered from his sniper training how important proper breathing is. He bent his knees adjusting his balance, held the weapon in both hands and aimed. He exhaled and fired. The target was twelve feet away and it swayed when the bullet struck.

That guy was lucky, Chase thought. His first shot was about two inches left of the chest. He repositioned himself and aimed once more. He emptied the magazine, shooting slowly and deliberately. All the remaining shots were in the body, but widely spaced. He lowered the gun and removed the head gear.

"Not bad for a first time. With a little practice we can make you competent. It was good that you went for the body. Anybody who says you should wound the bad guy in the arm or leg is full of crap.

"When you make the decision to fire you've passed the point where you're worried about taking a life. If you hesitate or are not willing to live with the consequences, don't draw your weapon. But, if you've determined that this person intends to kill you, you have to think exactly the same way. It's either do or die at that point."

"Got it."

"Proficient shooting has to be second nature. No thinking, or as I know they taught in Sniper school, controlled breathing. You may not have time to take a breath. It becomes reaction, totally."

"Understand."

"Put on your earmuffs. I'll show you what I mean."

Chase put on his headgear.

Les loaded his gun and stepped up to the start block. "Don't try this to wound someone." He drew his gun and fired off two of the quickest shots Chase had ever seen. Holes appeared in the left and right ear on the target. He didn't even take a stance or seemingly aim. He just pulled the trigger.

He smiled and fired two more shots. Another hole between the eyes of the target. Both bullets had penetrated the same spot. Then he emptied his last two directly in the center of the heart area. A point Chase had come close to only once.

"That takes years of hard work. For you now, don't worry about accuracy so much. Just repeatedly hitting center mass. Lesson one over. You're covered for any time you want to come back and throw some lead. You can shoot here for a while longer. Any questions just holler."

He left and Chase watched him saunter over to an attractive brunette firing at a target on Station 10. The shooting exhibition Chase just witnessed boggled his mind, nothing short of amazing. Les was truly one of a kind.

Chase spent another half-hour getting the feel of his

EMP. On the fifth target, all his shots were within the three smaller center circles. One was even in the center area. Not dead center, but close.

Chapter 16

A visit to a hardware store took over an hour but all items on Chase's list filled his plastic bags. He hurried back home, anxious to finish his refurbishing job. Surprisingly, he enjoyed driving the Hummer. It had plenty of power when needed and handled surprisingly well.

He pulled up the driveway and angled back to the three-car garage as raindrops sprinkled the windshield. The Hummer narrowly fit into the left stall. The middle spot designated for the Mercury and the third housed the fishing boat when it needed repair or cleaning.

The front of the Mercury's area housed a fully operational work bench. Every tool necessary for home repair, vehicle maintenance, or woodworking had been stockpiled. Eric, the guy who had worked here previously, a mechanic and craftsman with wood, or metal fabricating, according to Beau, would be impossible for Chase to come even close. His ability in pretty much every one of those categories lacked expertise. Thank goodness for googling.

He pulled out the dolly and loaded the supplies he'd gathered. The fifty-yard path to the back of the house paved with asphalt made it easier to haul. He had to make two trips.

In the built-in shelves, he stored MRE's, canned soups, vegetables and fruit, various sizes of batteries, a first aid kit, blankets, plastic forks and spoons, paper plates and three burner phones. Then along the left wall he stored four cases of bottled water, a portable power station with USB port capability, three LED battery-powered lanterns, and three air mattresses. A small, metal table went against the right wall where he stacked cooking pans and a portable cooktop.

A folding card table and four chairs in the middle of the room provided a place to sit but could be stored at night for sleeping space. Two handguns, ammo, and mace dispensers took up space in the left corner as well as an additional vital container of forty-eight Travel John disposable toilet packs.

Chase had purchased two heavy duty brackets. They were essentially metal claws that he attached to the inside of the hatch, one on each side. When the four-inch by four-inch beam of solid oak he'd obtained was fitted in the clamps, the door could not be pulled open from the outside.

The safe room now officially stocked and secure, he went to gather everyone for a tour.

****

Lettie sat at the kitchen table with a bowl of green beans in front of her when Chase entered.

"Where's Char, Lettie?"

"I believe she's in the office payin' some bills."

"I finished the safe room and I want to show it to you both. Be right back."

"I'll be here. Somebody gotta snap these beans."

Chase scooted down the hall before Lettie tried to shame him into helping her. He found Char at the office desk, typing on the computer keyboard.

"Char I want you to see the safe room. It's all done."

"Minute." She held up one finger and continued pecking away. She finally jabbed the send button. "There. All paid up. Had to nudge a couple of Beau's clients to ante up so we could cover our payments this month."

She grinned at Chase and wrestled an unruly strand of blonde hair back behind her ear with two fingers. A constant battle that the hair always won.

Chase offered his arm. "Let's grab Lettie and go see what it looks like."

"Sure." Char hugged his arm and they headed to the kitchen.

"I'm glad you're here, Chase. Beau took Lily's passing hardest of all. You've been able to give him renewed focus. I hope you realize just how much he admires and respects you."

"Feeling's mutual. Beau is one of the smartest, kindest, and most generous people I've ever known."

"Well, you're the son he always wanted and never thought we would have." She squeezed his arm. "Me, too, darlin'."

They reached the kitchen where Lettie was placing her bowl of beans in the fridge.

"Ladies, after you and on to the safe room." Chase swept his hand toward the door.

They crossed the veranda and climbed down the steps into the yard. Turning left and walking about six paces, they stood in front of the entrance.

"I want you both to pay strict attention to what I'm going to say. This is a serious matter. I don't know for certain if it will happen, but two men have stated their intent to do me harm. If this comes to pass, this room will save your lives. That goes for storms, threats, whatever.

Consider this your earthly salvation."

"Mr. Chase, I'm prayin' that don't happen." Lettie smiled.

"Nothing wrong with prayer, Lettie, and I thank you for that, but I don't imagine the Lord would think that taking precaution is foolish either."

"Got that right, sure do." Lettie clapped her hands.

"First off, Char, see if you can open the door. Just pull up on it."

Char stepped up and tugged on the handle. It came up about a foot but she had to let it go. It banged closed.

"It's heavy, but I think I can do it." She heaved once more and this time it swung open.

"Lettie, you try."

She grabbed the handle and opened the door with not much effort.

"Lettie, you are the official door person. You're in charge."

She snorted a laugh. "Do I get a doorman uniform?"

"Don't think that's necessary. Okay, let's go inside. I'll go first."

Chase climbed down the steps and turned on the lantern.

"Wow, you really fixed this nice, Chase." Char swirled a complete circle, taking in everything.

"I wanted it to be livable as well as functional. We have cooking, sleeping, and hygiene supplies. The four of us could survive in here for three to four weeks. That won't happen but if you're gonna do something, might as well do it right."

"How serious do you think this threat is, Chase?" Char sat in one of the folding chairs at the card table. Lettie sat as well.

"From the police report and phone call I got, I have to believe it's a strong possibility. These men are thugs and have no problem resorting to violence. So, yes, I believe it's real. That's why this is here.

"You two and Beau will stay here if those guys show up. I'm trained to handle situations like this. And I want to be sure you are safely tucked away so I can concentrate on them and not be worried about any of you. That's why I agreed to live here. I'm here to protect you."

"Should we be scared?" Char squeezed his hand.

"We should be cautious and watchful. Report any unusual or odd occurrences. And we'll take no chances. From now on none of us will go anywhere alone. Now look around and see what's here and where it's located. I'll give Beau the tour when he returns."

Chapter 17

"Man, the motels in this city are ridiculous. Almost two-hundred bucks a night. More than three nights would wipe us out of our expense money."

Drew scrolled through the listings on his cell. "Wait. Here's one just off I-10. Hundred bucks. Cheapest I can find."

"Get it on the GPS. I'm tired of driving and I could eat an entire cow."

"Got it. Motel 6 in Sulphur. Stay on I-10."

Twenty minutes later they pulled into the motel drive and parked at the front entrance.

Dewey crawled out of the Charger and stretched. "Oh, man, every one of my bones just cracked."

"Yeah, that was a long haul." Drew looked at his watch. "Not bad though, ten after six. Let's see if they got a room."

They walked through the sliding doors and crossed the checkerboard flooring. Dewey stood in front of the huge six next to the 'We'll leave the light on for you' slogan on the signage hung on the counter. A young woman entered data on a keyboard at a desk next to the counter, and looked up.

"Welcome, gentlemen. Be right with ya." She resumed tapping the keys. Dewey guessed she was early twenties. A nice figure and deep green eyes were hard to miss. Dressed in light blue T-shirt and slacks, the six emblem on the shirt was difficult to read due to the curves under it.

Dewey leaned on the counter with both arms and looked at her. "I was just telling my brother that they have the prettiest women in Louisiana. Thank you."

She raised both carefully lined eyebrows. "Thank you? For what?"

"For just like that," he snapped his fingers. "proving me right." He smiled.

"Okay, I appreciate the compliment. Bet you want a room, huh?"

"Pretty and smart. Yes, ma'am, we'd like a room. For three nights. And we're just poor boys from up north so could we get a discount?" Dewey rested his chin on his hand and grinned.

Drew stood to one side slowly shaking his head.

"Sorry, but unless you're a senior, which I don't believe you are, or military no other discounts are available. You military?"

"Nope. Guess we don't qualify."

"I've got you in 122 on the right side of the building. One night paid will hold your room for two more days. That be credit card?"

"Cash. We pay cash." Dewey pulled out his wallet.

"With tax that'll be one hundred twelve dollars and ninety cents."

Dewey extracted a hundred and a twenty and handed the bills to her. While she opened the cash drawer he asked, "Any good place to eat around here?"

She counted out the change. "If you go north from here on Ruth Street, you'll find lots of places to eat. Turn right. All are pretty good. Can't go wrong." She smiled.

"If you wasn't workin', I'd sure love it if you could

join us."

"Shucks, I'll be here till ten." Thin, lavender painted lips twisted into a devilish smirk.

"Maybe we could go for a drink later?"

"Maybe." She did a slow swing from side to side.

Dewey gave a two-fingered salute and turned to go.

Drew chuckled as they walked out to the car. "You always amaze me, bro."

Chapter 18

Dewey woke up with the sun streaming directly into his eyes. "Cripes, shut the blinds, Drew. Drew? Aw, where are you?" He stumbled out of bed and yanked the cord. The room darkened and he rubbed his eyes. "Drew you in the bathroom?' No answer. "Where the hell did you go?" He grabbed some clean clothes and headed for the shower.

A few minutes later Drew opened the door and yelled, "Dewey, I got coffee!" He heard water from the shower, so he took a cup to the bathroom. He rapped on the shower door and Dewey stuck his head out. "Yeah?"

"Got coffee. Here on the counter."

"That's where you went. Thanks." Dewey turned off the water and stepped on the mat. He lifted the Styrofoam cup and sipped. "Ugh, nasty stuff."

"Yeah, but it's hot and black and best of all, it's free. It'll wake you up. You were dead to the world this morning. What time did you get in last night?"

"More like this morning. 'Bout two, I guess."

Drew raised his eyebrows. "So, you hooked up?"

"I never kiss and tell." He flipped his wet hair back and began to towel off.

Drew snorted. "Now that's a whopper. You always tell."

Dewey smiled. He finished toweling off and took another swig of coffee. "Let's just say I like this little berg." He spat into the sink, "'cept for the coffee. Let's find some grub and plan our day. We got some reconnoitering to do."

****

At breakfast the twins made their plans.

Drew pointed his fork at Dewey. "You remember what Miguel said when he gave us this guy's name? He's former special forces. Two tours in Iraq. Won't be a pushover."

"We just hafta be careful. That's why we brought the rifle. We stay away from him. Can't use any of that special stuff if we stay a good distance away. Besides, we know some stuff, too. We handled those four in Memphis, didn't we?"

"Sure did. They didn't know what hit 'em. I got the address in the GPS, ready to check the layout. We get this done tomorrow and we can do some partying here in town before we head to Memphis to pick up Miguel's product. Piece of cake."

"One thing though, Drew. I want this piece of garbage to know who's taking him out and why. We owe it to Donnie. Then he can rest in peace."

"Yeah, only right."

They finished their meal and hurried back to their room to change clothes. They dressed in water-repellant camouflage pants and shirts and heavy work boots, anticipating it would get messy while staying out of sight.

A light rain began to fall as they crossed the parking lot to their car.

"You know, this bright blue car is gonna stand out like a highway billboard. We ought to see about something less flashy. Maybe some old pickup. It'd have local plates as well."

"Oh yeah. Good thinkin', Drew. We can find something appropriate; I think."

They cruised Ruth Street and passed a barricaded entrance where a construction crew was busy adding a third floor to a new office building.

Dewey pointed. "There, that crew ought to have a likely target. See if you can find where their vehicles are parked. Don't see any here."

Two blocks down Drew nudged him. "There, that parking lot. Several possibilities."

Three older trucks, their beds packed with construction materials, sat under overhanging tree branches. They pulled into an empty slot, close enough to check out the surroundings.

Drew rolled down his window for a clearer view.

The lot was empty of people. Toward the back of the lot two vans with 'Thompson Construction' logos took up four spaces. The three trucks they were interested in had no signage and were at least ten years old, obviously well used.

"Let's just relax for a minute and take in the scenery." Dewey turned off the engine and they waited.

Five minutes passed. Nothing moved. The ticking of the cooling engine the only sound inside the car. Then a heavy door slammed shut. A short muscular man appeared from behind one of the Thompson trucks and walked over to a dark green Ford F-150. One of their target trucks.

Dressed in jeans and a wife-beater T-shirt, he rummaged in the bed of truck. He jammed an LSU baseball cap backward on his head, adjusted his ponytail in back, and then popped on a yellow hard hat. He pulled out a toolbox from out of the passenger side, grabbed a brown paper sack and closed the door with his right leg. They watched him stroll out of the lot headed in the direction of the office building without a glance at the twin's car.

Drew smiled. "Well, we got our tools and lunch and we're going to work."

"Just perfect. Wait a couple minutes in case he forgot something then we'll pick us up a pickup. Has a nice ring to it, don't it?" Dewey held up his hand for a high five.

No one entered the lot while they waited. "Let's see what we got." They climbed out of the car and walked to the truck.

"You stand here in back like you're getting something, and I'll get it started. Then take the car back to the motel and I'll follow." Dewey headed to the driver's door. One minute later, the truck kicked over, and Drew returned to their car. They met at the motel ten minutes later.

Dewey pulled into the space next to the Charger and got out. "You get the stuff out of the trunk, and I'll grab the rifle in the backseat compartment. I think there's room enough in the cab to stow everything."

Fifteen minutes later their transfer of equipment completed they tossed some of the construction supplies into the trunk of Charger and entered the Thibodeaux address into the truck's GPS. The rain spat down a bit harder as they entered I-10.

Chapter 19

"GPS says turn at the next road, Drew."

"Okay. I don't see anything but trees and bushes, do you?"

"Nope."

Ten minutes ago, they'd exited I-10 and followed a narrow asphalt road through a swamp. The trees overhead drooped over the road. With the now steady rain, the older wiper blades failed to keep the windshield clear.

"There. See it? Looks like a path more than a road. Turn in and let me check the map." They pulled onto a dirt path and after pulling farther off the road they stopped. "We should be about a mile from the place. Better leave the truck here and walk in. Less chance of being spotted."

They climbed out and Drew slipped on the wet grass beside the path. "Wish it wasn't raining." He pushed the floppy fishing hat he'd found in the bed of the pickup further down on his head.

"I think this is the way. The house should be to our right. Let's see how close we can get."

They hiked south.

"Crap." Drew snapped.

"What?"

"Water's runnin' down my back. This hat's like a funnel pouring inside my shirt. I hate swamps."

"Not so fond of 'em myself." He smacked the side of his neck. "Mosquitos are makin' a meal outta me, too. Look at the size of that one." He held out the carcass for Drew to see.

"I got a herd of 'em around me as well. Maybe the rain will drown 'em."

Every so often, their boots got so heavy they had to stop and dig mud out of the ribbed soles. Twice they waited while a snake slithered off the path in front of them.

"That's one of the other things I hate. Snakes." Drew shivered. "Give me the creeps."

"We ought to be getting close. Keep a look out. We don't want to stumble out into the open where we can be spotted."

Drew continued in front of Dewey, mumbling about the nasty conditions. He swatted a low hanging branch out of the way, and as it swung back, it slapped Dewey on the forehead.

"Ow. Watch it. That got me."

"Oh, sorry." Drew turned back and stared. "You okay?"

"Yeah. But watch when you mess with the branches. They sting when they hit you."

"Yeah, I'll be more careful." He turned and marched forward. Then he stopped. "Wait. I think I see something. Yeah, looks like a building. Up ahead."

Dewey eased up beside him. "I see it." He crouched down and spread apart the tall grass. Looks like a cabin. It's on stilts. I thought his in-laws had a huge house. This isn't it. Maybe someone else lives around here." He pulled out his binoculars. It's a good size house but it isn't a mansion."

"See any movement?" Drew spit out a piece of grass that had swarmed into his mouth as he squatted next to Dewey.

"Nothin' yet. Let's watch it for a while."

Chapter 20

Chase dismounted his exercise bike and toweled off. Due to the rain, the thirty-minute workout inside substituted for his fast walk through the trails around the property. That avoided the possibility of messing up his knee by taking a tumble on the muddy terrain.

He much preferred the outdoors rather than listening to some over-achieving professional instructor on a TV screen. He could never find anyone on the bike's monitor who was pleasant and relaxed enough for him to listen to. He always turned off the unit and enjoyed the scenery out his back window.

When describing her home, Lily always had a dreamy look on her face. She was not only a gifted doctor but had excelled in her English minor at Northwestern. She had an affinity for spouting words he'd never heard before. She wouldn't just say that the trees standing around the bayou were a bluish color. She'd said they were caesious. He laughed recalling his snort when she uttered the word.

Her face had flushed, "What's the matter?"

He'd been caught between seeming ignorant or giving her the impression that she was speaking down to him. "I just never heard that word before. What does it mean?"

"Oh, sorry. Bad habit of mine. It means bluish or grayish green. It seems the perfect picture word for the bayou." She grinned and he fell that much more in love with her.

Chase finished his workout and showered. He was ready to complete a few more minor repairs on the inside of the Thibodeaux home. Locking the door, he went to get the ATV and go to work.

Chapter 21

"What's he doin?"

"Just a minute, Drew. I'm lookin'. He's leaving, looks like. Going to a shed in back."

"Is it him? Anderson?"

"Hard to tell. 'Bout the same height but his hair is different and no beard. Could be him if he got cleaned up. Can't be sure though. Wait. He's climbin' on a ATV. Yep, he's leavin'."

"Comin' this way?"

"No, heading east."

"Let's go check out the house. Maybe we can verify who it is."

"Give it a couple minutes to make sure he's leavin'."

"We need to leave here, now. I just heard something move in the grass. And it wasn't nothin' small. I'm goin'." Drew stood and studied the grass to his right. "Some critter's in there. I know they got crocodiles crawlin' all around. I'm outta here."

"It's gators, dummy. They have gators not crocs. Let me put my binoculars away."

They crept down the path. When they approached the end of the tall grass Dewey pulled up sharply. "Whoa. Look at that. There's the mansion. Down there."

"Wow. That's big. So, since that guy's headed up there, I think we can assume it's Anderson."

"Sure looks that way." Dewey let the binoculars

hang by the cord around his neck. He slowly turned completely around.

"Okay, east is the big house. You sneak up there close as you can get without being spotted. See who's there and what they're doin'. I'll go west to find a good spot to set up a mini camp."

"Got it."

"And use your ear buds to talk. Keep it to a minimum."

"Right. I'll give it say fifteen minutes. Then I'll call with what I see."

"Great." Dewey headed through a narrow path away from the stilted house. The bushes and trees provided good cover, helping keep some of the rain from further soaking him.

The path paralleled the bayou. He tried to accustom himself to the unfamiliar sounds of the swamp. The rain pelting the bayou surface, the diving of an animal or fish under the water, the swirling grasses on both sides as he made his way deeper into the swamp. And all sorts of animal noises. So different than the constant bustle of Chicago.

He kept glancing back to make sure the stilted cabin was still visible. He leaned on a tree trunk to dig mud out of his shoes once more. Each boot seemed to weigh twenty pounds apiece.

Then a small, cleared area about four feet wide about fifteen feet from the water's edge leading back into the swamp appeared in front of him. The space reached as far as he could see through the undergrowth. Perfect. Kneeling next to the stump of a downed tree, he lined up the binoculars toward the house. About 600 yards he estimated.

"Dewey, it's me. Can ya hear me?" His ear buds crackled.

"Yep. How's it goin'?"

"Oh, just peachy. Damn mosquitoes are havin' a ball. I may need a transfusion when we get back all the blood I'm losing. I almost stepped on a big black snake a minute ago. I love this place."

"Quit gripin'. It's not like they aren't here, too, ya know. What do ya see?"

"I saw the woman with white hair. Haven't seen anybody else. She was shakin' something off the porch. Like a rug or blanket, then went back in."

"That's probably the mother-in-law. Keep a look out. Found a place to stake out the other building. Can you stay hidden well enough if Anderson comes back?"

"Yeah. Got a pile of dead tree limbs to hide in. Looks like somebody stacked 'em away from the house. Got a good view."

"Stay there. I'm going to check out the house back here. Let me know if he heads this way."

"Oh shucks, why would I do that? It'd be great to go ahead and take him out when he gets there."

"You forget. We left our weapons in the truck. This is a reconnoiter not the termination part."

"Oh, yeah. Forgot. I'll alert ya if he heads your way. I'll be glad to get a hot shower after this stupid rain. I don't get this soaked when I go swimmin'."

"It's supposed to stop this afternoon. Don't sweat it."

"Too wet to sweat."

"Shut up. I'm goin' to the cabin." Dewey walked back down the path to get a look at the stilted house.

Chapter 22

Chase hauled his toolbox into the kitchen and placed it on the floor near the back door. "Good morning, Lettie. I'm ready to install that spice rack for you."

"Awe, mornin' Chase. That'd be so nice. Mr. Beau got it for me because he saw me always tryin' to find a certain spice I need." She resumed loading the dishwasher with breakfast dishes.

"That was nice of him."

"Not really. Helped him more than me. I'm always rummagin' around in those cupboards cussin' and bangin'. He said maybe he can get some peace and quiet now around dinner time." She grinned.

"Okay, I get that." He looked around. "Where is it?"

"Oh pshaw, I forgot I put it in the dining room next to the buffet."

Char came in from the veranda dragging an oriental rug. "Hi, Chase."

Lettie rushed over and grabbed the rug. "Char, I told you I'd get that rug for ya."

"Lettie, I may be retired, but I'm not in a wheelchair yet. I'm still going to help out around here."

"Doc told you to not over-exert yourself. Goodness you just had your back surgery a couple of months ago" She rolled the rug up and stomped off. "I'm gonna put this back in the foyer."

Char yelled after her. "Don't treat me like a feeble

old woman,"

Lettie waved one hand and mumbled something neither of them could make out.

Chase smiled at Char. "She's got a point. The doc did say to be careful."

"I was a nurse for twenty-four years, so I know about doctor's instructions. Had enough of them to last three lifetimes. He said thirty pounds max for three months. That rug weighs about twenty pounds. Not a big one."

"But you were shaking it and that is a lot harder on your back than just lifting. Just sayin'." Chase hurried into the dining room to retrieve the spice rack before she could respond.

Lettie returned and Chase carried the rack into the kitchen. "Where would you like me to hang this, Lettie?"

She looked at the rack and then around the room. "How 'bout on the side of the pantry? Would it fit there?"

Chase held it up against the side of the oak wood cabinet. "Looks like it's a perfect fit to me. If that's where you want it, that's where it'll be. I'm going to go get some heavy wood screws. Need something sturdy to hold this up. Be back in a bit."

He strolled out the back door and headed to the garage to search for the screws in the tool bench. Chase loved the way the bench was outfitted, like a hardware store. Screws, nuts, bolts, and fasteners of all sizes for metal or wood projects were neatly arranged in bins. If he couldn't find it there, it wasn't going to be found anywhere.

After a successful hunt he returned to the kitchen.

"Got some screws and a couple of brackets. I'll have this thing up in no time at all."

"Great, Chase. Can't wait to fill it with my spices. It'll be a joy to be able to find what I need without a hassle."

"Without the cussin', too." Char chuckled.

"You got that right. I do get upset when I know what I want and can't dig it up."

Lettie finished loading the dishwasher, Char wiped down the cabinets and dining table while Chase installed the spice rack.

Fifteen minutes later, Chase stepped back and waved his hand toward the rack now in place. "There you are, Lettie. Ready to be filled with your secrets to good cooking."

"Oh goodness, Chase. Thank you. And the one Beau picked out is one I would have chosen myself. You did good puttin' it up." She patted his shoulder. "I'm loadin' it right now."

"When you get done, I need to talk to you and Char. We'll sit down with a cuppa coffee for a few minutes."

Char tossed her cleaning rag on the kitchen counter. "Sounds serious, Chase. What's going on?"

Lettie rummaged in a drawer next to the refrigerator coming up with five spice jars. "Yeah, we can talk while I'm stockin' the shelves."

"Ok. With this possible trouble, I want to know how familiar you both are with weapons. Especially handguns. Char, you first."

"Daddy was a hunter. We often went huntin' turkey and deer when I was growing up. Had my own .22 rifle at thirteen. Not a bad shot. Then when I got married Beau liked to hunt and he also had me take a few sessions with a handgun. A Colt 1911 he has. I'm afraid I'm more reliable with a rifle."

91

"Good. What about you, Lettie?"

"Like Char I grew up huntin', but ours was for food. Daddy let me fire his rifle a few times. He didn't like to waste ammunition. Guess that says how good I was, don't it? Far as a handgun, nope. Only time I handled one was when I found one of Beau's in a closet I was cleanin'. He almost had a heart attack when I handed it to him and told him I didn't want to see that thing ever again. I had my hand wrapped around the handle and he thought I was gonna fire the dumb thing."

"I remember that." Char laughed. "He was sputtering so; I couldn't understand what he was telling me."

"So, the Thibodeaux army is somewhat handicapped in the weapons department. I'm going to set up a small target range out by the big woodpile. I piled it so dense a bullet won't get through. We all need to practice.

"Now, ladies, this is just a precaution. I have no idea whether these Chicago thugs will show up. After all, it's just a rumor right now. I'm betting they won't, but I always say it's better to be prepared than not."

Lettie let out a sigh. "Chase, I don't want to have anything to do with a pistol. I'm too scared of 'em."

"Lettie, you're going to be our rifle person. No handgun."

"I can do that. Yes, I can." She nodded her head rapidly.

"Char, do you feel comfortable shooting a pistol?"

"I can do that. But I don't know if I can actually shoot a person. Definitely something I'll have to think about."

Chase saw confusion in her eyes. "Absolutely

correct. Guns are a last resort. If it comes to that, it means someone is here to hurt you. They'd have no hesitation shooting you. At that point, you're saving a life and it may be yours. I'll not lie to you, it'll change your life forever."

"I'm going to visualize that whoever is comin' at me is a big old, wild boar wantin' to do me harm. Them things are nasty." Lettie shook her head.

Chase chuckled.

Char nodded. "Now that I can do as well. Daddy stopped one of those in back of our house when I was a teen. Weighed almost a hundred pounds. We ate good that winter. Amazing how fast those suckers can run."

"When I get the range set up, we'll have our first session. And make sure you know exactly where your weapon is so you don't have to stop and think about it. I want it to be like second nature in case of trouble."

Chapter 23

Drew slapped a mosquito that had landed on his cheek. "Dewey, can you hear me? Testing 1,2,3."

"I hear ya. How's it goin'?"

"Damn bugs are everywhere. I kill one and four more show up. I'm gettin' some bug spray when we get back."

"Well, your voice is loud and clear. Too loud. Don't have to yell for me to hear you. Rub some mud on your face. That'll help with the bugs."

"I ain't puttin' none of that nasty smellin' stuff on my face. Have you smelled it? Like rotten eggs."

"Suit yourself. What do you see?"

"Bugs, trees, mud. I'm behind that pile of dead trees they got stacked up. I got a clear view to the garage and the north side of the mansion. Haven't seen anyone yet."

"All I've seen is that old lady shakin' out a rug or something, and our boy when he walked to the house. I looked inside that place on stilts. Looks like that's where Anderson is living. So, we could get at him from this south side.'

"Sounds like a plan to me. How long we gonna stay here?"

"We need to find out for sure how many people are in the big house. Don't want to do our job and have six or seven people come runnin' out maybe carryin' weapons. Can't have this be a mass murder site. Then we got big trouble."

"Wish there was a way to flush everyone out so we could do a count and get outta here. Between sweatin' and bleedin' I'm losing lots of body fluid."

"Just hang in there. It could be hours."

"Just peachy. You know what happened a minute ago when I took a leak?"

"No, but I'm sure you're gonna tell me."

"Let's just say those mosquitos don't care where they land."

Dewey snorted. "There's always the mud, bro."

"Wait a minute. A car's comin' down the drive. Big old Merc. Old guy driving. I'm guessin' father-in-law."

"Stay out of sight."

"Like I'm gonna stand up and yell, 'Hey look, here I am'. Chill, got it covered."

"Whatever. Let me know if you see anything else."

Ten minutes later Drew whispered, "Dewey. Dewey. I gotta move."

"What's the problem?"

"He's coming this way. I'm movin'."

"Who's coming? Drew?"

"Just a minute," Drew whispered again.

"What's happening? Damn it, answer me." Dewey heard Drew grunting and panting.

"Okay, I'm out of the way now. Anderson came out of the back door with what looks like a toolbox and headed right for the woodpile. I had to move quick. Don't think he spotted me."

"What's he doing?"

"Messin' around in front of the pile. Not sure. He's nailin' stuff to the wood. Can't see what."

Chapter 24

Chase returned to the house after setting up the target range. He set his toolbox next to the back door and entered the kitchen. Lettie was wiping down the counter.

"Anything else I can do for you while I have my tools handy?"

Lettie looked up and smiled. "Can't think of anything right now. But I'd like to talk to you for a minute if you have time."

"Sure, Lettie. What is it?"

"Let's go to the veranda. It's nice to sit under the canopy and watch it rain. I love it out there."

"Deal. Let's go."

Chase headed out the back door, holding it open for her, while Lettie grabbed a tray from the counter. She thanked him as she came outside and placed the tray on the small wicker table between them.

"I wanted to properly thank you for putting up my spice rack. So, I made some of my famous pecan tarts. And a cup of coffee for you, too."

"Wow, Lettie, thanks. You know how I love those things." He took a tart and began to peel the wrapping from the bottom.

Lettie took one and sat down. "It's great to sit out here and listen to the bayou." She leaned back and swept her hand toward the river. "Lots of folks think the swamp is a nasty, smelly, mud-filled garbage pit. I don't. To me it's a reflection of the world. There's some dirt and filth but also serenity and fabulous beauty."

"Since I've been here, I can see why Lily always got teary-eyed when she described it to me. She shared your love for this place."

"Lily was my sister. Not literally course, but we just clicked, you know? I haven't said so yet, but I am so sorry for your loss. There was no one like her. She was gonna to make a name for herself. And she would've been a fabulous mom."

"Thank you, Lettie. I'm still grieving, and I don't know if I'll ever stop."

"My momma always said, 'when you lose someone special a piece of your heart is permanently damaged but joyous memories help smooth the jagged edges.' I cling to that philosophy."

"I like that. You had a smart momma."

Lettie laughed. "She never thought she was smart 'cause she left school after the seventh grade. Had to work to help the family survive."

"I've known some really dumb people who have a college education. And I know some people, like your mom, with no college who are very smart. There's a difference in education. On the one hand, book learning is put on too high a pedestal. Learning about life and every day existence is much more important. If I had to rely on book learning, I'd be totally lost."

"I hear ya. I've been so blessed to be here with Beau and Char. They have both kinds of education. That's why Lily was so good. They passed it on to her." She crossed her legs and began to swing her bare foot.

Chase took a sip of his coffee. "It is relaxing to sit here and listen to the sounds of the bayou."

"Cajuns believe the swamp is a living thing. It breathes and grows. Always changin'. Many of us have never known anything else. Seems it gets under your skin."

"Us northerners agree but the things that get under our skin are mosquitoes." He slapped his arm.

"Don't seem to bother us. Probably some scientific reason that I don't have a clue about. My education was more literary."

"Where'd you go to school?"

"Graduated from LSU with a degree in elementary education, with a generous helping hand from Beau and Char. Was going be this wonderful teacher of young people. Had all kinds a plans to teach here in Lake Charles."

"Why didn't you?"

"Short story of a long dark period. During college I met a guy. Smart, fun and patriotic. He joined the service right before we got married. He did three tours in Iraq and was killed by a sniper two months before he was due to get out."

"Oh, Lettie, I'm so sorry."

"Was a while ago. We never had much time together but when we did it was heaven. Had a son who was just as headstrong as his daddy. But he didn't find the right kind a friends. Doin' time for armed robbery. Unfortunately, one of his partners killed a clerk and it became hard time. He'll be middle-aged when he's released."

"Do you get to see him often"

"Not much. He's too embarrassed to have his mom visit. Too ashamed. He allows it on some holidays. Can't be very happy occasions for him. I cry for days after each visit." She wiped away a tear.

"I'm sorry. Here this is supposed to be a relaxing time and I'm messing it up something fierce."

"You couldn't know. I don't talk about it a lot."

"I should've stopped the conversation earlier. I apologize. I enjoy talking to you."

"Me too. You're easy to talk to."

"You know, I've been wanting to see a movie and get a meal but hate to go by myself. Would you want to do that sometime?" He held up both hands. "Not a date or anything, just two people who want to get out and not feel alone."

She studied him for a moment. "Yes, I think I'd like that. Done it by myself a couple a times. Couldn't wait to get back home." She smiled, dimples appearing.

"We'll make it happen. Now, I gotta have one more of these tarts."

Chapter 25

"Drew, we got a little problem here."

"What?"

"Anderson just sat down on the back porch with a woman. Don't know who she is. Younger than the other one I saw. Good lookin', too. They're eatin' cupcakes or something."

"Wonder who she is? Didn't see anything in our research about another woman. Cupcakes? That reminds me, I'm getting' hungry. Why don't we go get somethin' to eat? Feel like a drowned rat. What's it been? Three hours?"

"Keep your shirt on. We need to find out who she is, and if she's visiting or livin' here."

"Well, I'm comin' over there. Nothin' goin' on here. Just wasting my time and fightin' critters."

"Okay. I'll keep watch."

"It'll take me about half an hour to backtrack and catch up."

"They're still sittin' on the porch. Wonder if he got a new girlfriend. Maybe we'll take her out and make him watch. Donnie would've liked that."

"Right now, I'd say do it and the quicker the better. I hate this place. I'm soaked, full of mud, and bug bites. Won't be happy till I see Louisiana in my rearview mirror. See ya in a bit."

Forty-five minutes later, Drew plopped down beside

Dewey.

"Took me longer than I thought. Slipped and fell four times on this crap. Gonna have to pitch these clothes. Never be able to get 'em clean enough to wear again."

"Don't sweat it. When Miguel pays us for his delivery, we can buy new ones."

"Great, and we'll be home again. I can smell the city instead of rotting swamp. Let me take a look through the binoculars. Wanna see what she looks like."

"Okay." Dewey handed them over. "They been talkin' on the porch all this time.

"Wow, she's a looker all right. Have you seen anyone else?"

"Nope, just her. So far, we got four people in there. Maybe she's a maid or something."

"Not dressed like a maid. Don't they wear a uniform?"

"I don't know. I never had one before."

"Wait a minute. The door is opening. The old man and his wife are comin' out."

"Let me see." Dewey jerked the binoculars out of Drew's hands. "Yeah, they're all shootin' the breeze." He lowered the binoculars. "The way I see it, our best shot at this guy is when he's at the cabin. We can grab him when he's away from the people at the big house."

Drew slapped his neck and looked at his hand. "Sounds like a plan to me. Sooner the better. Before these guys finish off their meal."

Dewey adjusted the binoculars once more. "They're just sittin' on the porch. Not doin' anything. I guess there's 4 of 'em total. We can come back tomorrow and grab the guy. Wait a minute. That phone Miguel gave us is vibrating."

Dewey dug out the cell. "Hey, Miguel."

The familiar raspy voice came through with static. "Is this Drew or Dewey?"

"It's Dewey."

"I see you're in Louisiana. What you doin?"

"Just chillin'. Enjoying our vacation."

"You need to remember to make that pick up for me. You got that?"

"No sweat, Miguel. We won't mess up. In fact, on our way down here we stopped in Memphis and found the dock where we take delivery. No problem."

"*Bueno.* That would be good. You know…good for your health. Number one job is that truck. *Comprende?*"

"We got it, Miguel. You can count on us."

"Maybe if you do ok, I make you our permanent guys. Steady work for you. You like that?"

"Oh yeah. That'd be great. We're on it for sure."

"Call me from Memphis. You gotta tell me what's goin' on. Keep me informed. Don't blow it."

"Will do."

Miguel hung up. Dewey shoved the phone back in his pocket.

Drew slapped him on the head. "What'd he say? What's up?"

"Everything's good. He's checking up. Says if we do this job right, he'll make us permanent drivers. Piece of cake job. Go where he tells us, pick up a load and bring it back. Easy work and we don't have to do any heavy lifting."

"Good, let's go. I'm tired of bein' the main course for every flying insect in this swamp."

Chapter 26

The veranda door creaked, and Beau and Char joined Chase and Lettie who were seated on the chaise lounge near the potted Ficus, watching the sun rise over the bayou.

Beau escorted Char to a cushioned chair and flopped down in the one next to her. "Thought we heard you two out here. What's goin' on?"

Lettie leaned over and shook her finger at Beau. "We was just tryin' to avoid you, ya old goat."

"Now, Lettie, you know you love being with me. Who else is such a willing target for one of your barbs?"

"Willing target my asphalt, pardon my French." Lettie sank back in her chair.

"And when were you gonna offer me some a those muffins there?"

"Since when did you ever need to ask for one? And they're not muffins, they're tarts. And I seem to remember once when I had a pan sittin' on the counter coolin' off, I got back and four of 'em were gone."

Beau licked his fingers. "They sure were good."

Lettie rose, scooped up the pan, and offered it to Beau. When he reached for a tart, she pulled it back, and then offered it to Char.

Lettie smiled. "Ladies first I always say."

Char took a tart. "Thank you, Lettie. I don't think he should have one. The doctor says he needs to lose some weight."

Beau grunted. "Aw one isn't gonna hurt."

Lettie shoved the pan toward Beau. "Since when did you ever stop at one?"

Beau grinned and took a tart in each hand. "I love your muffins, my dear."

"Two of 'em isn't gonna shrink that gut any." She replaced the pan and sat down.

Chase looked up, shading his eyes. "Sun's getting high. Looks like it's gonna turn out to be a nice day. When it dries out a little, I'm going to do a walk around the property."

"Want some company? Apparently, I need some exercise." Beau glanced at Lettie and took a bite of his tart.

"Got that right." Lettie patted her belly and pointed to Beau, spreading her hands wide to signify a beach ball size.

"Would love the company, Beau. I'll show you the target range I fixed up. We can go out there anytime and get some practice in."

"Should I gear up?"

"No, not yet. I want to make sure our wood pile will stop bullets from causing harm down the road."

"Okay, let me know when you're ready to go. I'll be in my office. Lettie, those muffins are a heavenly treat. Thank you."

Lettie's eyebrows raised. "Tarts! You're welcome. Must have put somthin' special in my recipe to make that man issue a compliment. I'm gonna find out what it was and order a semi load of it."

Everyone laughed and Beau turned beet red.

An hour later Beau and Chase walked down the long

driveway toward the wood pile.

Beau stopped and took in the view. "Ah, I love this place. My soul, our soul, Char's and mine, are buried deep here. I still feel Lily is around keeping watch on us. I hope you do, too."

"She often said that she was only half a person in Chicago. The other half was here."

"My hope is that eventually you'll feel that as well."

"Beau, if I'm not there, I'm awfully close. I've healed here. You literally saved my life. Without Lily, I was ready to die. But you and Char, and Lettie, have made me feel alive and wanting to find purpose."

They continued their walk.

"Let me ask you something, Chase. All these preparations, like we're creating a fortress almost. How much of a threat are we facing?"

They'd reached the woodpile.

"Truthfully, I don't know. I've never been one to be overly cautious, but I think it'd be foolhardy to ignore a possible threat. One that the detective from Chicago made a special effort to warn me about."

"I hear that. Seems to me this whole world has taken a turn to self-destruction. I see it in my practice. Some of my clients who have committed violent acts have no heart. No emotion, no shame about their actions. I'm glad I'm retiring."

"Yes, it's a different world all right. I still wrestle with my actions. I'm ashamed of what I did, but I don't regret it either. I couldn't let that man go free to cause pain to anyone else. I know it'll never be resolved in my head.

"Overseas in combat, that was different. I knew it was either my enemy or me. Self-preservation. No rationalization needed. But, if that man's brothers are seeking revenge, in some convoluted way I understand."

"I was never in the service so I can't relate. Some of the stories from clients and relatives, though, are heart breaking."

"Every soldier has had to re-evaluate his or her value system and reconcile it with the stark reality of war."

"I never thought of it that way."

"Then when we re-enter the normal world, some have trouble with the adjustment." Chase swept his hand toward the target range he'd fashioned. "So, I've made a place for us to practice self-preservation. In answer to your question, yes I think we could be in danger and I'm going to do everything in my power to protect us."

"Thank you, Chase. I'm really glad you're here."

"Not me. Don't get me wrong. I love you guys and am so grateful. But I brought this problem with me, putting you in danger. That haunts me. I don't even want to think about something happening to any of you. It would be the end for me."

Beau swiped away a bee hovering near his nose. "Chase you're part of our family, and we'd accept nothing else than for you to be here. No matter the consequences."

"Thank you for that." Chase pointed to the ledge he'd fashioned in front of the woodpile. It held twelve split logs with concentric circles drawn on the front of each. "I've set up these pieces of wood at normal chest height. You can come out and practice at your convenience. Like I said, it's better to be prepared than not. When the ladies come here, I'll be with them to help."

"Looks good. I'll do my part."

Chase walked to the right side of the ledge. "I want to make sure our practice shots don't go any farther than the pile."

Logs about two feet in length stacked six feet high stood behind his ledge. He estimated it to be at least two cords of wood. Between the ledge and logs, uncut tree limbs four deep waited to be chopped for firewood. He continued around the back of the pile and stopped.

"Beau, come here."

Beau hurried around to join him. "What is it?"

Chase pointed to the ground on the left side of the pile. "Boot prints." He knelt down. "And here, these impressions, looks like someone knelt here watching the house. Let's get back."

They left and quickly headed to the house.

Beau limped on his bad knee and tried to keep up. "You think it's those brothers?"

"Can't imagine who else would sneak around."

"Could they be taking aim at us now?"

"If they had an idea about shooting us, they had better opportunities as we were coming out here. I'd guess they're checking to see what they're up against."

"Should we alert the sheriff?"

"We could let Tony know what we found, but we can't even be sure who made the tracks. Could be some local stopping for a rest on his way to fish or hunt. And we don't know when the prints were made for sure. Although they look fresh from the rain."

"I'll give him a call. He's already increased his patrols around us but he hasn't got enough deputies to really give us much help."

"I'm going to put you, Lettie, and Char in the safe room and do some investigating."

Lettie sat on the porch alone when Chase and Beau returned.

"Lettie, please go to the safe room. We'll join you there." Chase pointed to the safe room.

She jumped up from her chair. "What's the matter?"

Chase waved at her. "Go on with Beau. I'll explain when Char gets there."

Lettie hurried down the steps, and she and Beau went into the room.

"Char where you at?"

"Here in the dining room, Chase. What's up?"

"We need to go to the safe room right now, please."

Char's eyebrows lowered. "Problem?"

"Don't know for sure but I don't want to take any chances. Let's go."

Char darted down the hall to the kitchen and out the back door. Chase pulled the door closed and locked it, then followed Char.

Once inside the room, Chase secured the door with the improvised door jam. He gestured for everyone to sit around the table.

"Beau and I found boot prints and indications that someone has been watching the house. We don't know who it was, or even when those prints were made, but I didn't want to have everyone separated and be unable to find one of you."

Lettie slapped the tabletop. "I'm ready for a fight. Bring 'em on."

Chase smiled. "We're not in a fight yet. I want you three to wait here until I get back. I'm going to take a look and see who, if anyone, is prowling around our place."

Char's eyes were teary. "You be careful."

"Don't worry. This was my job for seven years overseas. I won't be gone more than say…" He looked at his watch. "one hour. Remember the code to open the door? Three soft taps and three louder ones. When I leave, bolt the door."

One hour later he gave the all-clear. He'd found additional tracks around the shack but whoever it was had disappeared. He was even more concerned with this discovery.

Chapter 27

Chase adjusted the headphones and took aim once more. The comfortable, padded ear gear he used when listening to his favorite jazz music worked just as well for target practice. A slight jerk as he fired did not affect the accuracy of the direct hit. His last rounds showed marked improvement. Thirty rounds shot with twenty-eight in the circle. Two barely outside.

He was satisfied with his fourth time at his new makeshift range. Practice makes perfect still applied. Also, he had few worries about the noise. The house was secluded, and hunters routinely frequented the swamp.

He picked up the spent shells and wadded up the damaged paper targets. One more time he inspected the area behind the woodpile searching for any new signs of unwanted guests. He saw none. On his walk around the house yesterday, he'd not seen any unwanted guests.

Chase holstered his Glock and decided to scout the property again. If someone was lurking around, maybe he could flush them out. Besides, he enjoyed the bright sun and mild temperatures of this April afternoon.

Beau and Char had gone into town on a "date" as they called it, for lunch and a movie they had wanted to see. Lettie was flitting around the house doing some of her spring cleaning, so he had no worries about his family's whereabouts if he happened to discover someone who didn't belong.

A huge eagle gliding overhead caught his eye. The bird swooped down to the river, and just above the surface extended its claws, quickly waving powerful wings angling up with a fish speared on its talons. He marveled at the beauty of that moment.

The light breeze showered him with the scent of jasmine. Chase veered west of his shack to venture deeper into the swamp. He headed up the path used by deer, racoons, other assorted wildlife, and the occasional human.

Chase settled into a steady pace alert for any unexpected encounters, human or otherwise. The longer he was here the more a feeling of peace and contentment seemed to settle on him. He wouldn't call it happiness, but maybe a sense of belonging. The deep pain of losing his Lily was still agonizing, but finally, he was able to enjoy recalling happy memories of their brief life together.

He no longer asked why God would allow someone so beautiful, both physically and spiritually, to suffer such a horrible and disgusting death. His faith consisted of experiences as a kid forced to attend church. He believed in God but was no a fan of so-called organized religion. Many of the Christians he'd known didn't act very Christian.

Chase talked to God but didn't classify it as prayer. Mostly questions which he never seemed to get answered. So why blame God when he didn't actually participate in God's religious world? For Chase the beauty of nature was something to believe in. And it did come from God, so he guessed that functioned as his religion.

He spent an hour wandering through the mossy

trees, lush vegetation and skittering creatures both seen and unseen. When he returned to the house Lettie had just stepped outside on the veranda.

"Hi, Lettie."

"You enjoy your walk?" She put her hands on her hips and bent backward. "I gotta quit bendin' over so much. My back is killin' me. Must be old age catchin' up."

"You're not that old."

"I'll be forty in a couple months. Sounds real old to me."

Chase smiled. "You are in your prime. Beau told me to enjoy these years because they don't last long and are the best of our lives."

"You can tell that to my back. Maybe it'll help."

"I doubt it will."

"You showed up too soon. I was fixin' a surprise for you. Now you're gonna spoil it. "

"A surprise? You want me to go take another walk?"

"Naw. Won't make no difference. Come on in. I'll show ya."

Chase followed Lettie into the kitchen and was immediately overpowered by a wonderfully sweet scent. "What's this?"

Lettie pulled down the oven door. "I'm fixin' you a birthday cake."

"Birthday cake? Oh my, I forgot my own birthday. Now we're talkin' old." Chase bent down and inhaled. "Smells divine. Thank you."

"Got to let it cool so I can ice it. I'll only put one candle on it. If I put all thirty-nine on there, we'd burn the house down."

"Thanks. Can't wait to taste it. And we certainly

don't want to burn down the house." Chase smiled and licked his lips.

Chapter 28

"Hurry up. Let's go. I wanna get this done and be on our way."

Drew shoved a fork full of scrambled eggs into his mouth. "Let me at least finish my breakfast. I'm starvin'."

Dewey snorted. "You always take too long to eat. I been done for five minutes."

"Have not. And you're still drinkin' your coffee. Have another cup and relax. We got plenty of time."

"I just wanna get it over with. It's like a big boulder hanging over my head, waitin' to drop. I feel like the road runner in that cartoon."

A bite of egg fell onto Drew's lap. He grabbed it and popped it into his mouth. "Piece of cake. We scoped it out. We're prepared. Not to worry."

"Yeah well, we got a plan A, but no plan B. What if something goes wrong?"

"Plan B is that we have two rifles. If I miss, which I won't, then you shoot. Simple. Keep it simple I always say." He finished his coffee.

"Just sounds to me like we haven't got it fleshed out all the way. Still worries me that this guy is a soldier."

"Ex-soldier. Ex. No soldier is going to be a problem if they're shot."

"I've seen it in movies. You see a guy shot and think everything is cool. Then the guy gets up and whacks the shooter."

"This is real life. It don't work that way. Remember the guy in Cicero? Was just wounded and he crawled around cryin' like a baby. It hurts. It hurts. He was screamin'."

Dewey picked up the check. "Okay. Let's go. Get it over with. Besides we're runnin' low on expense money."

Drew pulled a dollar out of his front pocket. "I'll leave the tip. She didn't give me my extra jelly for my toast." He threw the bill on the table, and they left.

Thirty minutes later they were back in the old pickup pulling onto the same dirt road they parked on yesterday.

The twins were again dressed all in black from boots to baseball cap.

Drew climbed out of the driver's seat and pulled the wires apart to shut off the engine. He walked to the back of the truck and unloaded his backpack and rifle and handed Dewey his. After strapping Glocks onto their belts they each unzipped their pack and pulled out headsets.

"Testing 1, 2, 3. Can you hear me now? I sound like that commercial. Can ya hear me now?"

"Sound is clear." Drew looked up at the sky. "Clouds'll give us some cover. That's good."

"Good if it don't rain."

"Not supposed to according to the weather report."

"And they're right - most of the time."

"Aw, quit gripin' an let's git."

They jogged in a half crouch down the path, rifles at the ready. Both men stayed to the left side of the path, walking in the short grass to lessen the sound of their approach and for quicker access to the taller grass for cover if needed.

Dewey stopped and pulled Drew back by the tail of his shirt. "Hold up just before we get to that place on stilts." He looked at his watch. "It's 6:30 so we should be here before Anderson gets up to the big house. Then we can grab him."

Drew slapped Dewey's hand off his shirt. "Okay, okay. I know plan A. Knock it off. And talk in your mic. That's what they're for. Crap." He turned and continued on toward the stilted house.

Chapter 29

Deputy Ron Withrow stopped his cruiser, then backed up to get a look at an old pickup parked several yards down a path leading into the swamp near the Thibodeaux place. He used his binoculars to search the area around the truck and focus on the license plate.

"Base this is X-10."

"Go ahead, Ten."

"Run some plates for me. I think I located that missing pickup. Louisiana MSN413."

"Got it. MSN413. Checking."

Deputy Withrow waited for a response. The red pickup parked on a path winding toward the bayou matched the description on his be-on-the-lookout list. He opened the squad's door and stepped out.

"Ten, we got a match. Do you need backup?"

"Not right now. Looks abandoned. Going to go check it out."

"Careful, Ten."

"Joyce, you know me. Always careful."

"Right, like the time you ran into three heavily armed poachers who decided they didn't want to be arrested."

He laughed. "All turned out fine. I carefully got the drop on 'em."

"Just take it easy. Call if you need help."

"Roger that."

The deputy unhooked the leather snap on his weapon and took one more look through the binoculars. Nothing. He let them hang in front of him and crept down the path with his hand on the handle of his Glock.

The truck bed was empty. He opened the driver door and looked inside. Bare wires dangled below the steering wheel. *Well, that's how they got it started.* Another look around the front of the truck revealed nothing either.

He squinted down the path. Foliage and ...there. Footprints leading back into the swamp. He knelt to get a closer look. Boot prints. Two distinct sets. Ron decided to go back to the car and get his shotgun.

"Base, X-10."

"Go, Ten."

"There are two sets of tracks leading into the swamp. No indication that they've returned. Could be back there right now."

"X-14 is close. I'll send her. Five minutes."

"I'll be here. Ten, out." He got into the squad and maneuvered it down the path to block the truck's exit. Then he settled back to wait.

Seven minutes later a second car arrived. Deputy Sharon Darnaud parked behind Ron's car and got out. Ron waved.

"What ya got?" She leaned on the open window of Ron's car. Sharon, a slender Black woman with curly black, shoulder-length hair tied below her trooper hat, smiled.

"Found that pickup. Two sets of footprints lead from the truck into the swamp. No sign they came back."

"Dang, you gonna make me get my uniform dirty again? County never paid my laundry bill from the last time. Took me two hours to get all the gunk off my boots."

"Can't promise a clean trip this time either. Sorry."

"Let me get my shotgun. Man, I was hopin' for an easy day today." Ron knew she was joking. Sharon, an eight-year veteran officer, had been a reliable, competent partner several times. He knew her complaining released tension and calmed her for whatever happened.

"Base this is X-10. Backup on scene. We're going to check this out."

"Roger. Be safe."

They started down the path, passing the truck. Sharon on the left, Ron on the right. Both crouched, moved forward, and carried shotguns barrel down.

Chapter 30

Chase finished his morning exercises and headed to the kitchen for breakfast. A bowl of cereal and some coffee seemed to be what he needed to jump start his day. Beau had mentioned a possibility of fresh fish filets for dinner, and they were going to get an early start to reel in three or four grilling candidates.

With the second cup of hot coffee in hand, he stepped onto the small back porch of his home. A typical gorgeous day in the bayou. The morning fog burning off under a bright sky, and a mild breeze lazily moved the moss-covered trees in a ballet of low hanging limbs.

Once again, he wished Lily could be here to enjoy it with him. He'd never get used to her death. Every time he took in the beauty of this place, her memory would be omnipresent. It both tore at him and relieved him that he could still vividly picture her. He never wanted her image to fade.

He pulled out his cell to call Beau. It caught as he tried to lift it out. He fumbled removing it from his pocket and it fell to the floor. When he bent to pick it up a shot rang out. He felt a shock wave as the bullet zipped by his head. Grabbing the phone, he scrambled inside.

Chase sprinted down the hall to the bedroom where his gun was. Pressing the speed dial for Beau, he mentally urged him to pick up quickly.

"Mornin', Chase. Ready to go?" Beau exuded

eagerness.

"Get Char and Lettie into the safe room. Someone just took a shot at me. Get yourselves safe. I'll handle this."

"Will do. Stay safe yourself."

He hung up and checked his weapon. The Glock had a full clip. He chambered a round.

The shot had come from the west. He debated whether it was a stray shot from a hunter or if someone was actually targeting him. A sense of foreboding washed over Chase. Washburn's two brothers and their threats popped into his mind.

Chase moved to the exercise room where he had a better view to the west. As he entered the room, he nabbed his binoculars from the cabinet as well as his rifle and a box of shells.

Next, he called 911. He scanned the area. No movement. He waited. The morning was unnaturally quiet. The shot had silenced all wildlife. Cornered in a small room only made him a sitting duck.

Chapter 31

"Damn! I missed. Had a clear shot at him on the back porch. Just as I pulled the trigger, he bent down to pick something up. Dewey, you see him?"

"No. I'm in front of the house. Can't see the back. I'll circle around and come at him from the east."

"Okay, hurry. We gotta get this done quick now. He's probably callin' the cops."

"I'm hurryin'. Gimme a minute."

Two minutes later, Dewey settled into position facing the east side of the cabin on stilts. "I'm there. Don't see him. Probably hunkered down. We need to flush him out somehow. Put a couple of rounds in the room on your side there. If he sneaks out on my side, I can get him from here."

"Okay. Shooting now." He placed three shots into the side of the cabin just under the window.

****

Three flashes about two hundred feet away pinpointed the shooter and Chase placed two shots a bit above where they'd appeared. The incoming bullets punctured the wall, just missing him. One embedded in the seat of the exerciser, tearing it off the cycle.

The other two plowed into the far wall, taking out a painting of a wolf Lily had given him on his birthday. Shifting farther right to the other side of the window, he still saw no one and didn't hear anyone moving around.

He decided to move to the other side of the cabin to sneak out and get north of the shooter. Maybe he could outflank him and get a better shot. Someone he could spot. If it turned out to be the brothers, more than likely two shooters would be aiming for him.

He crawled into the kitchen and eased open the sliding door.

For a good two minutes he lay flat, watching and waiting. Then he heard two shots. Pistols. Two more shots quickly followed. Shotguns.

Sounded like the war had followed him to Louisiana.

****

"Dewey, I'm hit. Got me in the shoulder by the collarbone. Can't move my right arm."

"Hold on, Drew. I'm comin'!"

Dewey ran in front of the cabin, not caring if he was seen or shot at. He had to get to his brother.

Drew lay on his back in a thick patch of grass, blood pooling under his shoulder.

"Hold on, Drew. I'll get you outta here." He knelt and took out a knife and cut away Drew's shirt near the wound. He wadded up the piece of shirt he'd cut off and stuffed it onto the shoulder to staunch the flow of blood. "Hold this tight as you can."

"Drop your weapon and put your hands up."

Dewey turned. A Louisiana deputy stood about one hundred feet from him.

Dewey placed his rifle on the ground and rose putting up his hands. "My brother's been shot officer. He needs attention."

"Where is he?"

"On the ground beside me." He jerked his head

motioning to Drew, and whispered into his mic, "Drew, can you reach your pistol?"

"I think so." Drew was breathing heavily.

"There's two cops. Can you see either of them?'

"I see one on the left and almost half the other one through the grass."

"Can you get the one on the right?"

"Think so."

"I'll take the one on the left as they move in. When I say three, we both shoot. Okay?"

The deputies began moving closer, shotguns ready.

Dewey pointed down. "Officer, my brother's bleeding badly. We need an ambulance."

Deputy Withrow clicked his shoulder mic. "Base, we need an ambulance at the Thibodeaux place. Gunshot wound."

"Three!" Dewey yelled.

Drew rose up and fired at the deputy to the right. Dewey dropped to a knee, drew his pistol and shot the other deputy, who fired a wild round from his shotgun. That deputy fell as the woman deputy shot Drew in the chest.

Dewey looked down at Drew. His chest was a mass of blood, and he instantly knew Drew was dead. He glanced at the two deputies. The man he shot was on the ground not moving.

The other one, the woman, swung her shotgun at Dewey from the ground where she had fallen when she took a bullet to the leg. Dewey shot her in the chest. She groaned and fell back. The cops would be there soon.

He had to get away. The two deputies were between him and the truck. He'd have to pass directly around them. What if they aren't dead? Sweat ran down

Dewey's back and forehead.

He crept closer. Both deputies lay still. The male's eyes were open but unseeing. He was sure that one was gone. The female deputy's eyes were closed. He knew she'd taken two bullets. He put another into her chest and took off running toward their truck. He needed to get away.

Sure didn't pan out the way we'd planned. Now both his brothers were dead, and he literally swam through tall grass in a mangy Louisiana swamp. Tears and sweat ran into his stinging eyes. This man he stalked would pay for the loss of the only two people in the world he cared about.

When he reached the truck, it had a cop car butted up against the back. He maneuvered the truck out through the grass around the car and back onto the road. He headed back to the motel to ditch the truck and retrieve their car. Anderson had escaped for now.

Dewey wasn't done yet though.

Chapter 32

For five minutes Chase squatted underneath his house, his head swiveling in all directions. No more shots were fired, and no one moved through the grass or on the gravel walkway. The shots had come from the east, so he headed that way, his rifle aimed slightly down but ready for any assailant.

The swamp remained quiet and eerie. The chest-high grass swayed gently in the breeze, and insects buzzed around Chase's head. A couple hundred yards in he spotted a pair of legs sticking out from the grass on the right. They weren't moving.

He crept up and found a man, dressed all in black, lying face up. His unseeing eyes and bloody chest clearly indicated death. Just to make sure, he checked for a pulse. None. Chase removed a pistol from the man's hand and tossed it away. A rifle lay in the grass nearby.

He continued on and a few feet farther another body lay sprawled on the ground. This one was a cop, also dead. Chase turned to scan the area and discovered yet another body on the opposite side of the path. A female cop, alive but unconscious.

Chase laid his rifle down and hurried to help the officer. Her left leg had a bad wound, still bleeding. He removed his belt and tied a makeshift tourniquet around the thigh just above the wound. He couldn't see any other obvious problems. Probably in shock from the trauma.

He pulled out his cell and made another call to 911.

"911, what is your emergency?"

"I'm on the Thibodeaux property with a sheriff's deputy who's suffered a gunshot wound to the leg. Need an ambulance ASAP."

"Sending one. What's your name, sir?"

"Chase Anderson. I live here. I called before about sending the police. There's been a shooting."

"We are responding. Six minutes out. Please remain in the area. Any other injuries?"

"So far I've found two bodies. One a male deputy and one an unidentified male. I'll stay here till help arrives."

He also called Beau in the safe room and filled him in on what happened. He cautioned him to stay there with Char and Lettie in case the killer might be still around.

Chase retrieved a couple of blankets from his home for the officer. One he used to prop up her injured leg and the other to cover her to keep her warm. Then he went back to the dead man he first saw.

A quick search turned up the man's wallet. Andrew Washburn. Lombard, Illinois. Washburn, he knew the name. Donnie's brother. Some cash and a piece of paper were stuffed in his front pocket. He unfolded the paper and saw an address in Memphis next to a date and time. He slipped it into his shirt pocket and then replaced the cash and wallet.

Sirens approached and Chase returned to the deputy. She was breathing shallowly, still unconscious.

EMTs jogged down the path and began assessing the officer's wounds, setting up an IV drip. They placed the wounded deputy on a gurney and rushed to the ambulance. A few moments later Sheriff Bernardo arrived with two additional deputies. The sheriff asked a few questions and then told Chase he'd meet him at the Thibodeaux house after he had the crime scene secure. Chase's cabin was now part of the investigation.

Chase slowly walked along the path to the Thibodeaux home. He called Beau and told him they could return to the kitchen. His mind filled with flashbacks of the shootout, questions about what to do next, relief that he'd not been wounded or worse. But someone tried to kill him. That plain made him mad.

Everything bunched together in a swirl of confusion, guilt that he'd brought violence to this beautiful place, fear for the safety of his family, and rage that one of the brothers was still at large. He had no doubt that this would not be the last he'd hear about the remaining Washburn.

As he climbed the porch stairs, Char burst out of the kitchen and bear-hugged Chase.

"Oh, Chase. We were so worried. So afraid the shots we heard would… You're not hurt, are you?" Her mascara ran in rivulets down her face. She pushed him into the kitchen and led him to a chair.

"No, I'm okay. Just shaken up."

"You want some coffee, tea?" Char hovered in front of him, dabbing Kleenex at her tear-stained face.

"Here's what he needs." Beau held a bottle of his special-occasion bourbon. He poured a generous amount in a glass and handed it to Chase.

"Let's not get him liquored up before the sheriff gets here." Lettie grabbed the glass and set it on the counter. "This calls for some Cajun coffee. I'll make some. What else can we get for you, Chase?"

"Right now, just a glass of water. The sheriff is going to be here when he gets his crime scene set up."

****

Chase, Sheriff Bernardo, and a State Trooper sat in Chase's living room an hour later. Beau, Char and Lettie were sequestered in the dining room waiting for the questioning to end. The coroner had removed the bodies and an investigative team had cordoned off the crime scene with fluttering yellow tape. Three uniformed officers searched outside for evidence. A local TV station cameraman and reporter stood outside the tape, throwing questions at anyone who walked by.

"Tell me what happened here, Chase." The sheriff asked. He and the trooper sipped the coffee Lettie had insisted must be made.

"Not much to tell, Sheriff. I was standing on my back porch when I dropped my phone. As I bent to pick it up a bullet flew by. I grabbed my phone, called 911, and went to get some firepower. More bullets hit the side of my house and I targeted the flashes.

"At first I thought it might be a stray shot from a hunter. But when additional shots came at me, I knew they were intentional. I went into self-preservation mode. I don't know who else would be wanting me dead. Gotta believe it's the brothers."

"Did you see the exchange with our officers?"

"No, I was hunkered down under my cabin. I heard two pistol shots then two reports from shotguns, then another shot a few minutes later." Chase sipped his coffee.

"How much time between the original shots fired at you and the final shots?"

"At most I'd say fifteen minutes. I spent a good five

minutes or so under the house trying to find a target."

The sheriff nodded. "The dead man was ID'd as Andrew Washburn. From Lombard, Illinois."

"His brother, Donnie, murdered my wife."

"We believe one other person escaped. Probably Andrew's brother, Dewey. Got an APB out for him now. We'll get him."

"How's the other deputy? Couldn't do much for her."

"Alive. Lost a lot of blood, but they think she'll make it. The tourniquet more than likely saved her life. Thanks. The other man shot her point blank in the chest twice. Her Kevlar vest stopped the bullets. But she'll be sore for a while."

He got up to leave. "We'll be in touch. More patrols will be assigned to provide what protection we can. Just be wary."

"Count on that."

Both men left and Chase took a deep breath. *Now what? There's still one brother left out there. Doesn't seem likely he'll stop coming after me.*

He remembered the paper he'd found and pulled it out of his pocket. Memphis Tennessee, two days from now and an address.

Looks like I'm gonna need to do some travelling.

Chapter 33

The truck they had stolen slid in the mud as Dewey tried to speed up. He corrected and fishtailed onto the road leading back to their motel. *Gotta get outta here. Donnie's dead, Drew's dead and if I don't move fast, I'm gonna be sittin' in a cell for a long time.* Sweat rolled down his back. He wished Drew were here to help make a plan. He couldn't believe how screwed up this got.

He failed to erase the vision of Drew's blood-covered body. Supposed to be a piece of cake. The road had light traffic so far, but it wouldn't be long before cops swarmed like bees to honey.

The first thing I need to do is ditch this truck somewhere. Oh Crap! I gotta ditch our car, too. They'll identify Drew and then the car registered in his name.

Half an hour later, Dewey parked the truck in a warehouse parking lot a mile from the motel. He wiped it down quickly and hiked back to their room. He took a quick shower and dressed in a Springsteen T-shirt and jeans. Once he had their gear packed, he hurried to the car and sped out onto the road.

The directions to free parking at the Lake Charles Regional Airport were clear and easy to follow. He breathed a sigh of relief that he'd seen no cops. An empty spot at the far end of the lot seemed perfect. He pulled in between a big Ford pickup and a GMC Envoy.

Hopefully, that'd make it harder to spot.

He punched the trunk release and eased out of the driver's seat. Stepping back to the rear of his car, he gathered his bags and closed the lid. For once he was glad Drew had insisted on a roller bag. He'd look like a regular traveler. He placed a smaller bag on the back of the car and pretended to check the insides. Now he would wait.

A few minutes later a Toyota Highlander pulled down the aisle. A pony-tailed driver held a phone to her ear and gestured as she talked. She turned into an empty slot six cars down from Dewey. She got out still talking on the phone, while the liftgate swung up. She was dressed in a dark blue business suit, with high heels. Two minutes later she stuffed her phone into her purse and began pulling bags from the car, a large suitcase, a heavy carry-on bag and a matching laptop bag.

She adjusted a pair of sunglasses from the top of her head to her nose, went back to the driver's door, and opened it. She retrieved a cardboard sunshade from the passenger side and positioned it under the rearview mirror across the windshield.

Dewey smiled as he again fiddled with his bag. Nice. She wouldn't find her car missing for a while. He watched the woman pull out her phone and resume talking. She couldn't gesture because her other hand tugged the luggage behind her. She entered the terminal and Dewey waited another five minutes to make sure she wouldn't return. Once he was sure no one else appeared, he jimmied open the door. He loaded his bags, then worked his magic to start the car.

Ten minutes later he guided the dark blue SUV to the highway. He still needed to make that delivery for

Miguel if he wanted to live. The heavy, fruity perfume smell forced him to open the window so he could breathe.

To take his mind off what had happened he turned on the radio. Country music blasted out threatening to make him deaf. Thankfully the lady had Sirius XM and he found a rock station. He settled in for the drive to Memphis at a cruise-controlled speed of sixty-five.

No need to hurry. He had two days before he had to pick up Miguel's load.

Chapter 34

Beau had never been able to mask his thoughts. They're written all over his face. He'd lose everything in a poker game.

"This is not a good idea, Chase. Let the police handle it."

"I think I know where Washburn's headed. If the appointment listed on this paper is important, he'll be there." Chase waved the paper he'd taken out of Drew's pocket.

"Then give it to the police. They can apprehend the guy."

"Do you really think they're going to act on a slip of paper?"

"Well, we won't know if you don't give it to 'em, will we?"

"Beau, this guy's not going to stop until he kills me. What if he escapes again? It'll be much harder to find him the next time. No, I gotta do this myself. That way I know he'll not come back. I'll be protecting you, Char, and Lettie."

Beau shook his head. "I won't condone what you're doing. Every instinct I have says this is wrong. I'm an officer of the court sworn to uphold the law. By you telling me what you're intending to do, I should report it as a potential crime."

Chase smiled. "No, you can't. You're my lawyer.

What I tell you is privileged."

"Son, there are all kinds of ways around that. But I can see that even if I report this you'll still go, won't you?"

"Yes. I refuse to let Washburn have another opportunity to hurt people I love. I promise I'll try to turn him over to the police, but if it's him or me, I choose him."

"I pray you can make that happen." Beau's eyes were moist. "We'll all pray for you."

"I appreciate any prayers. One favor I ask."

"What?"

"Can you drop me off at the rental place? I need to rent a car."

Beau smiled. "Now you're asking me to participate in a crime?"

"I can't ask to borrow either of your cars. They'd stick out like a sore thumb."

"For sure. When do you want to go?"

Chase checked his watch. "It's just after five. I'll grab a bite to eat, then we can go. I reserved a car; they close at seven. My bag's already packed."

An hour later, Chase thanked Beau and assured him he would call and keep him advised on his progress. Beau left and Chase entered the rental place. A businessman leaned on the counter while the Agent Harper, according to her nametag, filled out paperwork.

"There ya go. You're all set. Have a good trip." Agent Harper smiled and handed over the keys.

"Thanks." The businessman picked up his briefcase and walked out the door.

"How can I help you?" Agent Harper asked. Her

uniform, a green and gray shirt, and matching slacks, fit nicely. Her pink hair was combed to the left and the right side of her head was shaved smooth. Four studs in her right ear glinted in the light. A nose ring and a safety pin in one eyebrow made Chase cringe.

"I have a car reserved. Name's Anderson."

She smiled and began to dig through a stack of papers. "Yep, I remember you called today. I think we settled on the Chevy Blazer. Here it is. Stall 7."

"We did." Chase noticed another piece of metal on her tongue. He wondered how she ate food. And he hoped she avoided powerful magnets at all cost.

"Do you want insurance?"

"Probably be a good idea," he answered.

When Harper finished filling out the paperwork, she handed him the keys and a folder full of documents. "There ya are. Have a nice trip."

Chase left the office and found stall 7. A silver Blazer filled the space. He stowed his bag in the back, placed a bottle of water in the cup holder, and settled into the driver's seat. He threw the rental agreement in the glove box.

He felt adequately prepared. His Glock and a Ka-bar knife in a sheath were on his belt. His bag contained extra ammo as well as a pair of binoculars, and a heavy-duty flashlight which had a taser available at the flip of a switch.

He took a deep breath and began the journey to Memphis.

****

Dewey couldn't keep his thoughts away from the mess in Louisiana. The image of Drew's bloody body refused to go away. Dewey tried everything to focus on something else.

Thinking about Drew also brought to mind Donnie. *Both my brothers dead. How could that happen? Anderson's gonna pay. Donnie or Drew either one will never rest if that jerk continues to walk the Earth.* He pounded the steering wheel twice in frustration. The screwdriver he'd stuck in the steering column fell out and rolled on the floor under his feet.

"Crap." He guided the car with his left hand and fished around the floorboard with his right. He had to bend down in his seat to reach all the way. Finally, he felt the handle and grabbed it. His movement caused the car to swerve left almost clipping a big Lincoln SUV passing him. The driver shook an angry fist at him.

Whew, that was close. Last thing I need is to try to explain to a cop why I have to use a screwdriver to start my car.

Dewey had decided not to travel on Interstate highways to be less conspicuous. Interstate highways equaled boredom. US 171 North wound through small towns and would help break the monotony.

He stopped at a small diner on the outskirts of Shreveport; he needed to find a route parallel to I-49 into Arkansas. While enjoying a really good plate of fried shrimp and hush puppies, he studied a map he'd swiped at a gas station.

Now to make the delivery for Miguel.
****

Chase passed through Baton Rouge and connected onto I-55 toward Memphis. Two hours into his trip and so far, he'd been blessed with light traffic. Even though the rented Blazer had Sirius XM the radio remained silent. He wanted to reflect and refine his plan to find

137

Washburn.

He expected the trip to Memphis to take approximately 5 hours, arriving around 3:00 p.m. local time. Lettie had made a reservation for him at a Memphis hotel Beau used for business trips. He'd have plenty of time to scout the place listed on Drew Washburn's note. The time for the meet a day and a half from now, Friday at 2:00 a.m., at the docks.

Chase had no idea what the meeting involved, but it didn't take a rocket scientist to figure it'd lead to criminal acts of some kind, an exchange of money for drugs, or other contraband. That would mean the presence of guards and additional armed personnel.

He didn't want to start World War III so he needed to stake out the place and find out where Washburn would go next. Then he could follow and determine a better place to confront him.

No amount of planning was ever perfect. Something always threw up unforeseen obstacles. His Delta training included the phrase, "plan A is invariably compromised, always have B and C ready." His supplies included adequate firepower and ammunition. He had no worry about that. All the other unknowns that he'd listed on his planning notes caused his apprehension.

How many others would Washburn be meeting? What if the man was leaving by boat? The list seemed endless.

Cruising at a respectable seventy miles per hour, Chase wondered what Lily would say about his journey. She'd definitely be against it. She hated violence - one of the reasons for her to go into medicine in the first place.

A dear high school friend of hers had been seriously

wounded by a stray bullet in a drive-by, a stray bullet in a Lake Charles neighborhood not normally known for random violence. The girl had lingered two weeks before succumbing to her wounds.

No amount of cajoling or rationalization would have convinced Lily that Chase's intent could be right or just. Even the main point of his pursuit, the safety and protection of Lily's family, would not have won her over.

Basic principle number one, that every life mattered, had no gray area. Any confrontation could be resolved by calm heads working out their differences. Even with war. They had agreed to disagree on this subject.

They'd had many conversations about his reasons for military service. Lily had read the reports of Chase's injuries. He saved the lives of two comrades from the IED that had shattered his knee. And even though wounded, had engaged and killed three terrorists in the encounter. She acknowledged that Chase deserved hero status but was sad to find he'd taken someone's life.

Now, Chase followed his instincts to keep Lily's family from danger. The same instinct that propelled him to save his buddies on his overseas tours. On another mission he had earned a bronze star for heroism, but he had declined to accept it. He insisted he didn't deserve it because one of his comrades hadn't made it back. Although seven marines had been saved by his actions.

He wasn't going to let a madman cause any more pain to him or those he cared about. He continued on to Memphis and what he considered his duty.

****

"Crap!" Dewey had been weaving behind a huge farm implement for the past six miles. Every time he swerved to go around, oncoming traffic or a yellow no-passing line interfered. He pounded the steering wheel once more and quickly decided that was not a good idea. His wrist still throbbed from the last blow. Maybe the decision to avoid the Interstates wasn't his best.

Finally, a stretch of road cleared allowing him to pass. Two miles later he came to another of the million small towns he encountered requiring him to slow to 35 or 40. *That's it. I'm going to I-55.*

Fifteen minutes more of narrow roads finally allowed him access to an Interstate ramp. He set his cruise at sixty-five, below the posted seventy mph speed limit, just to be extra safe. He settled back and let out a long breath, not realizing how tense he'd been driving on the off-roads.

Realistically, most of his tension probably came from the shootout back in Louisiana. He still couldn't believe Drew had died.

How'd everything turn to shit after all his planning? So weird Anderson had ducked just as Drew had fired. Twilight Zone to be sure.

Once I get Miguel's truck and deliver it, I'm back to Louisiana to finish what we started. Hate leaving things undone. Don't worry Donnie, and Drew. I'll take care of business. You can count on that.

Three hours later, at 4:05 p.m., the Memphis skyline loomed ahead. A light rain had followed him for the last half hour. Bumper-to-bumper traffic inched along till he found his exit. He followed the GPS directions to the docks.

Fullen Docks and Warehousing had an exit directly off I-55. Dewey drove up to the gate. A short, skinny dude in a FDW baseball cap and dark blue coveralls with the FDW logo on the sleeve stepped out of the tiny gatehouse.

"Afternoon. What can I do for you?" His clothes and hat dripped water from the steady rain, and his full handlebar moustache wiggled as he talked. It hung down below his chin on either side and looked like someone had draped a large nightcrawler under his nose. Drew might have asked the man if he knew of any good fishing spots around. Dewey smiled at the thought.

"I'm just verifying this address. I have to pick up a load tomorrow and trying to get my bearings, so I don't mess up." Dewey gave him his best friendly smile.

"I hear that. What you pickin' up?"

"Here's my bill of lading. Getting' a load of Gulf Shrimp for a restaurant in Chicago."

"Oh, I love shrimp. Let me see." He studied the papers. "Warehouse Number 6. Down this road take the first left. Just past a stack of containers. You can see 'em over there." He pointed to a grouping about a half mile away. There must have been a hundred fifty piled four high next to the road.

Dewey thanked him and pulled away. He found the warehouse and drove around back. Several trucks parked at the loading dock where workers busily loaded trucks on one side and coupled containers onto truck cabs on the other.

Miguel had sent a picture of the truck and license number to Dewey's phone. No sign of it yet. He still had two days before his scheduled pick up.

Satisfied that he could find his way here and be at his designated spot on time, he headed back to find a place to stay. Maybe he could enjoy some nightlife while he waited. Although it wouldn't be as much fun without

Drew.

****

The whip-wamp of the wipers did little to erase the bug smears on the Blazer's windshield. Cars and trucks whizzed by eerily close. Chase hadn't driven long distance on an Interstate for years. The rain and smudge-filled glass made him nervous.

The GPS map showed 8.7 miles to his hotel, and he couldn't wait to get inside and relax. Later he'd visit the docks to determine his next move. The directions he'd taken from the dead brother indicated a time of 2 a.m. on Friday, in a day-and-a-half. He had to make sure he arrived early to spot Washburn. But first he'd check in, take a hot shower, and get some food.

The seven-story blue Hyatt Centric dominated the downtown block, not too far from the docks. Chase pulled up and parked in front. He checked in and located the weight room, restaurants, and pool. He'd take advantage of those tomorrow but first he wanted to get the car gassed and the windshield cleaned. Best to be prepared for a long drive if need be.

His plan would develop on the fly. His service motto was "Prepare for the worst." Something unforeseen always seemed to happen in every plan.

He'd made good time to Memphis, a little over six hours. After a shower and a quick lunch, just past 1 p.m. he left to check out the docks.

Twenty minutes later the car was gassed up and had clear visibility. He pulled up to the gatehouse at the docks and lowered his window. A short, mustachioed man stepped out.

"Yes, sir. What can I do for you?" Rain dripped from the bill of his baseball cap.

"I'm here to see about some warehousing. Something close to the docks."

"Came to the right place, mister. You need to talk to Charlie Winters. He's Warehousing Coordinator. Head down that road on the left. 'Bout a half mile a small building with a sign that says, Office. Can't miss it."

Raindrops escaped the end of a handlebar mustache onto the man's clipboard. He either didn't see them or ignored them. The papers on the board had a cellophane sheet covering for protection.

"Thanks." Chase waved goodbye and drove off.

Thankfully the warehouses he drove by were numbered. He located number 6 and pulled around to the back. A parking area off to the left had three empty spaces and Chase chose one. The tinted windows of the Blazer kept him concealed. He could observe and not be seen.

Chase counted eleven trucks loading out of the back of the warehouse. About half the people walking around had blue uniforms and hardhats with FWD logos. The other half were probably truck drivers - casually dressed and easy to pick out. His Atlanta Braves' baseball cap, jeans and T-shirt would fit in well.

He kept the windows up to avoid the diesel smell permeating the area. The two-story warehouse had a single window to the right of a small door which opened onto a metal walkway halfway up. At the side of the building a metal fire escape ladder hung down from the walkway. Chase filed that away for later. It'd be a perfect observation post to watch for Washburn.

Chase watched for another two hours. He thought he'd seen enough to get the lay of the land, so he decided to leave. Three trucks had completed loading and pulled out. One more banged closed and tagged. He followed that last truck out, and when they reached the gatehouse Chase pulled around and onto the I-55 ramp.

He drove back to the hotel and thought about a plan of attack. No doubt taking Washburn out at the warehouse would be too dangerous. Too many people and he didn't want any innocents to get hurt. If Washburn intended to pick up a load more than likely it was nothing legal. Probably would be guarded. He'd wait till Washburn left and follow him, then he could figure a better way for an ambush.

Nothing left to do but wait. Once back in his room, Chase ordered room service and watched the Braves beat the Mets. He'd done his share of waiting in the service and during rehab. This time it would be a piece cake. Raspberry. That was the dessert with his meal.

Chapter 35

"Who's this? Drew or Dewey?" Miguel Desantos sounded angry.

"Dewey. What's up, Miguel?"

"I have not heard from you for more than a day. I tried to reach you this morning and you didn't answer my call. You're supposed to be available to me anytime."

"I'm sorry. I had a situation and wasn't near the phone. We'd left it in our truck."

"Situation? What kind of situation?"

"My brother and I got into an altercation. He was killed and I escaped."

"Don't tell me you can't pick up my delivery."

"No, no. I got it. Some cops ambushed us when we tried to take out Anderson."

"Anderson...is this the man who killed your brother?"

"Yeah. Drew took a shot at him, then we were interrupted by a couple of cops."

"*Mierda Santa!* You have the cops after you? You bring them onto me?"

"No way. The two who attacked us are dead. It was them or us. We're good. Hey, my brother is dead. I had to leave him. Soon as I get back and turn over the delivery to you, I'm gone. I'm going back and kill that guy."

"Dewey, if the cops find me and I lose my shipment,

you won't be able to leave. You'll be dead."

Dewey explained in more detail to Miguel what had happened, describing Anderson and where the shootout occurred.

"Don't worry. There's no way they can connect me to you. I'll make the pickup tomorrow morning just like we planned and bring it to you."

"I think you would be smart to do that. I'm making a change. Hold on a minute." Dewey heard Miguel speaking to someone. A couple of minutes passed. "There will be three men at the pickup who will follow you to Chicago. They will be driving a black Camaro.

"I didn't want this to happen. It's easier for the cops to spot a shipment with a guard car following. You drive cautiously and do nothing to draw attention to yourself. If you mess this up, your brother won't be the only one who needs a casket!" The phone went dead.

Gee, that went well. How can things get so screwed up in just a couple of days? Dewey's whole world seemed to be crumbling. Now he'd be wanted for a shooting in Louisiana. He had some planning to do. Change his identity and his looks. He couldn't go back to his apartment. The cops would have that staked out. No, he needed to become someone else and leave town. He patted the key in his pocket. Fortunately, that key opened a storage locker containing the brothers' emergency kit - a stash of money and weapons to help create a new Dewey. Then he'd hightail it out of town.

****

Chase packed his bags and left his room at 9:30 p.m. He wanted to be at the docks by 10 p.m. to make sure he was ahead of Washburn. With little traffic he made it in under twenty minutes.

Three trucks waited in a short line to be logged in at the gatehouse leading to the docks. Chase pulled in behind the last truck. He didn't know what he'd say to be allowed through. He could see the gate guard give directions to the first driver.

Chase waited as two cars pulled in behind him. Then they pulled out around and passed his car and the trucks without checking in. Must be workers, Chase thought. The guard didn't even glance at them so, he decided to make like a driver and pull through as well. No problem. Guard didn't even look his way.

He drove to warehouse Number 6 and headed around back. The parking area contained six cars and three empty spaces. He parked in one and settled down to check out the activity.

Four trucks were being loaded. None of them the one described on the note. A total of eight dock workers loaded cargo inside the trucks. Steady rain beat down on the hood of his Blazer. Not too heavy but enough to create a rhythmic pattern. He had four hours to kill.

His backpack carried his 1911 EMP with two full magazines, his knife, a six-pack of bottled water, a box of power bars, a small jar of peanut butter, a box of saltines and a black plastic bag. He wanted to be able to move quickly once Washburn left.

Chase guessed Washburn's destination would be Chicago, so a five-to-seven-hour trip seemed likely. He planned to get up on the walkway and hunker down under the plastic bag. If this meeting dealt with illegal product, they'd probably check out the parked cars to make sure no one was watching.

Ten minutes later only three trucks remained, and they were at the far end of the dock away from the escape ladder. He seized his best chance. He grabbed his plastic bag and gently closed the car door. He locked it manually to avoid the beep of the key fob.

He walked over to the ladder and checked the area. He hoped it wouldn't screech when he lowered it. Luck was with him. It glided down smoothly, and he climbed quickly. He pulled the ladder up after him and hurried to the door leading into the warehouse's upper floor. Neatly piled next to it six boxes were covered by a tarpaulin. He squeezed in front of the boxes and draped the plastic bag over himself.

It wasn't the most comfortable place he'd ever hidden in, but it beat those he'd used as a sniper in the service. He could still taste the ever-present bits of sand and dirt that invariably found their way into his mouth.

He double checked the EMP 1911 in his holster and patted the two extra mags in his pocket, then settled in to await Washburn's arrival, hoping he wouldn't need to use them. He thanked his lucky stars for the spotlight over the doorway pointing to the lot. He would be almost impossible to see in his perch in the direct light.

****

Dewey drove past the gatehouse to the warehouse. He parked next to a black Camaro and climbed out. The dashboard clock registered 1:45 a.m. and under a single overhead light he spotted only one truck being loaded. The loading dock was locked up tight except for the white panel truck with 'Hagarty's Restaurant Supply' written in script on the side. Three men passed boxes inside in assembly-line fashion.

Three other men carrying rifles surrounded the truck, heads swiveling toward Dewey as he exited his stolen Highlander. He wiped the insides with a disinfectant cloth, grabbed his screwdriver from the steering column and his duffle bag. He walked over to the truck and eyed the three guards. They lowered their weapons after he showed them his papers and ID card.

"How's it goin, guys?" Dewey smiled.

No one answered. The men had hooded ponchos covering them from the rain. All were about the same height with faces mostly hidden. With beards and little light, he couldn't get any sense of what they looked like.

One of them motioned with his rifle toward the driver's door of the truck. "Get in. Almost loaded. Jaime will ride with you, and we follow in the black car." His rifle swung over to the parked car.

Dewey opened the door and stowed his bag behind the driver's seat. He got in and checked to see where the lights and wiper switches were and the gauges. The key was in the ignition. Kind of refreshing to be able to drive something and not worry about the screwdriver falling out. After adjusting the seat, he watched as they closed and locked the back door. The three loaders left, and one man climbed into the truck.

The passenger removed his poncho, stuffing it behind his seat and climbed in stowing his rifle under the seat

"Jaime, nice to meet you." Dewey smiled and stuck out his hand.

Jaime looked at Dewey's hand and turned away. "This ain't no party and we ain't gonna be friends. Drive."

Oh boy. Gonna be a boring trip. They buckled up. He put his left hand on the steering wheel and turned the key with his right to start the truck. As he pulled away from the dock the Camaro followed.

His non-friend wore dark blue jeans and polo shirt and smelled like garlic. His long hair dripped water down the collar, wetting the tattoos on the man's neck. The man crossed both heavily tatted arms over his chest. Looked like he was wearing a long-sleeved shirt.

Dewey passed the gatehouse and turned onto the I-55 ramp. He set the cruise at sixty-eight and tried to find a comfortable position in the seat. His back hit the cushioning wrong and he could find no lumbar setting. Great.

Jaime belched and the garlic smell worsened. Dewey couldn't wait till the guy farted. Then again, yes, he could.

****

Chase moved his legs again trying to prevent cramps and stiff joints. The rain seemed to be easing a bit but still pelted him with enough to create puddles on his plastic bag. The bag only covered his head down to his waist, so he had to tuck his feet up close to his body to keep his clothes from being soaked. His butt hurt from sitting on the metal walkway.

He peeked at his watch. Almost 1a.m. and activity at the dock continued. Eight men transferred boxes into five trucks backed into the dock. Ten minutes later four of the trucks pulled out heading who knows where.

Six workers gathered up gear and walked over to the parking area. They piled into their cars and left, while a black Camaro pulled into one of the vacated spots. Three men got out, donned hooded ponchos, and gathered at the trunk. Each man pulled out a rifle and partially concealed them under their outerwear.

"Amateurs," muttered Chase. They didn't check their loads. The men leaned against the Camaro and lit up cigarettes.

The last truck pulled out clearing the dock. The two remaining workers sat on the edge of the dock seemingly oblivious to the rainfall. Of course, they were already wet from loading, so it probably just felt good to take a break.

It didn't last long. A white panel truck arrived ten minutes later with Hagarty Restaurant Supply emblazoned on the side. It backed up to the dock and a short man exited and walked over to the three by the Camaro. They had a quick discussion and the short man waved to the two dock workers, motioning for them to come inside.

None of the men were Washburn. Where was he? Would he miss his meeting? According to Chase's watch it just reached 1:45 a.m. so there was still time for him to show. And three minutes later he did. A blue Highlander pulled into the spot next to the Camaro and Washburn jumped out. He rummaged around inside and pulled out a duffle bag. He walked over to the three men and showed them some papers.

One of the three pointed toward the truck with his rifle and Washburn climbed in the driver's seat. The man spoke to Washburn, lifted his rifle toward the Camaro and he and a second man walked to the Camaro. The remaining man removed his poncho and stowed it and his rifle in the truck and climbed into the passenger side.

The truck with the Camaro following, left the dock.

The two men who had loaded the truck returned to their cars and took off. Chase watched the Washburn convoy roll slowly past the gatehouse and head to the I-55 ramp. He waited till the last car rolled out of sight, stood and stretched his aching legs and arms.

It felt good to stand up again. He hurried down the escape ladder to his car. Washburn wouldn't be hard to catch up to. An important question remained, what would he do when he did catch up? He'd have to find an opportunity and react. And hopefully one would come before Washburn reached his destination.

****

Dewey wiped his eyes once more. Rainwater flew in his half-open window splashing his face. The truck's windshield wipers also threw water into the window. It seemed the only option Dewey had to keep from gagging on Jaime's garlic odor. The man must eat garlic smothered food each meal.

"Look, Jaime. We're gonna be stuck in here for at least the next four hours. I'm goin' nuts from boredom."

"Your job is drive. Mine is lookout. Nothin' says we gonna be best buds. Just drive."

The guy just sits there and oozes smells. Dewey had tried several times to engage Jaime in conversation. Either he couldn't speak English well or wanted to be silent. When Dewey turned on the radio, Jaime shut it off and gave him a look that said leave it off.

Dewey wrestled with the thought of putting a bullet in the guy's head. His Beretta still uncomfortably rested under his belt at his back. An hour and a half into the trip they finally moved past the rain.

Jaime dug his phone out of his pocket.

"Jerman, we need to trade places. This man is nuts. He wants to be my friend, I guess. We're gonna stop at a gas station at the next town. You like to talk. Talk. I am tired of his shit." He slid the phone back into his pocket.

Dewey looked over at Jaime. "Jerman?"

"Jerman talks a lot. Miguel's nephew and he will

talk your arm off. You could be asking for me to come back maybe. Take the next exit and find a gas station. Not a big one, smaller. Less cops. I need to pee."

Dewey said nothing. At least he might be less bored, and this trip might move along faster. He passed a sign announcing the next town six miles ahead. Taking that turnoff, he headed to the small town of Steele, Missouri.

They passed a Pilot and a couple of newer name-brand stations. Jaime motioned to a two-pump station on the left side of the potholed road displaying a poster that promised competitive prices but didn't specify on what. Dewey pulled in and angled into a spot in front of the office. The Camaro parked next to them.

Dewey and Jaime climbed out and stood next to the truck. The two guys in the Camaro got out and joined them.

Jaime pointed to one of the men from the Camaro.

"You get to ride in the truck. This guy wants to talk. I don't." He headed into the station. "I'm gonna go pee and get somethin' to drink."

The other man from the Camaro followed Jaime. "Me too."

Jerman stepped up next to Dewey. "My name's Jerman. Let's get in the truck."

The blank expression on his round face pretty much mirrored Jaime's as he got in on the passenger side. His pock-marked cheeks surrounded a nose that had been broken more than once. Clean shaven except for a fuzzy goatee that grew more fully on the left side, his jaw appeared to have something crawling on it.

Dewey shook his head. "I'm gonna get a drink myself. You watch the truck?"

Jerman nodded. "Go ahead."

Dewey entered and wandered through the snack aisle and grabbed two Snickers, then moseyed over to the glass encased wall announcing Beverages. Five panels displayed a wide variety of drinks. Dewey pulled out two Red Bulls and went to the partitioned cashier area. Jaime and the Camaro guy were arguing over a lottery ticket purchase.

"Let me tell you. Last week by using my method I won a thousand bucks. It works."

"Maybe I not go in with you then. My own choice works. I will get tickets for me."

"Whatever." Jaime put a handful of Oreo cookie packages and a six pack of beer on the counter and rattled off a string of numbers for his lottery tickets."

Finally, Dewey got to the counter to pay. Jaime and the other guy stood by the door loudly talking over each other in Spanish. He couldn't make out what they were saying with his limited Spanish vocabulary but by their expressions he could tell they weren't having a friendly discussion.

Good the beer would be in the Camaro. Riding with open beer cans on the Interstate isn't a good idea. But with the firepower those guys had he wasn't about to interfere.

He just wanted to get this over with.

****

Chase moved to the right lane once he saw the Camaro's blinker light flash. The two vehicles exited toward Steele, Missouri. *This may be my chance to do some damage.* He followed onto the ramp.

The pair bypassed the first filling stations instead choosing a small two-pump structure. Chase drove by and did a U-turn to come from the back side. He watched as the two men in the Camaro got out and stood by the truck. The two inside the truck also got out and they talked for a couple of minutes. Then two of the guys walked into the office and not too long after, Dewey entered behind them. The remaining guy climbed into the truck.

Chase turned into the entrance drive and pulled up three slots to the right of the Camaro. The fourth guy in the passenger seat of the truck seemed to be playing a game on his phone. Perfect.

Easing out of his car, Chase pulled out his Ka-Bar knife and carried it upturned with the blade resting against his arm for concealment. The parking area was deserted except for him. He walked up to the trunk of the Camaro, quickly bent down, and jabbed a small hole on the inside of the rear driver's side tire.

The man in the truck had not moved, still immersed in working with his phone. Chase walked slowly back to his car, grateful the car had tinted windows. He got inside and buckled up. It wouldn't take long on the highway for the tire to lose air. All he had to do was wait till they discovered they had a flat.

Just two minutes later, the three men left the station and got into their respective vehicles. The small caravan entered the Interstate and Chase followed several car lengths behind.

Eight miles up the road, the Camaro's turn signal began blinking. It pulled to the shoulder with the left rear tire clearly flat. Leaving a space of about a quarter mile, Chase pulled over as well. He watched the two guys in the Camaro jump out of the car and stare at the tire. The driver kicked the tire and screamed a stream of curses.

The men in the van joined the two and they began shouting at each other. One of the men threw up his hands and moved to the back of the car. He punched his key fob, and the trunk flew open, then he rummaged around the inside of the trunk. Finally, he lifted an armload of equipment covered by a blanket and hauled it to the backseat of the car. Chase had no doubt the blanket concealed weapons.

Washburn said something to one of the men and they began arguing. After both men pointed at each other nose to nose, Washburn gave the man a one finger salute and casually walked back to the truck and climbed in the driver's side.

The man he'd confronted went back to helping remove the spare tire from the trunk. All three gathered at the rear of the car and began changing the tire.

Chase pulled out his phone and dialed 911.

"911 emergency."

"I'm driving Interstate 55 just north of Steele, Missouri. Just spotted a car and truck pulled over changing a tire. They are all armed with rifles. Four of them."

"Rifles? Are they shooting them?"

"No, they took the guns out of the trunk and put them in the backseat of the car. Late model black Camaro."

"Can you safely stay around to talk to an officer?"

"No ma'am. I'm outta here." He hung up.

Chase sat back and waited for the police to show up.

Chapter 36

Miquel's nephew, Jerman, seemed okay to Dewey. He did like to talk, and they had exchanged stories about themselves already. Dewey had just told Jerman about his adventure in Louisiana when Jerman's phone chirped.

"What?" He swiped a loose black curl from his eyes.

"A flat? Bro, that's a new car. Tires got less than five thousand miles wear."

"Okay, we're pulling off."

Jerman replaced his phone in his pocket.

"We gotta stop here. They got a flat tire. Find a good spot to put on the spare."

Dewey signaled and pulled onto a patch of asphalted shoulder. The Camaro pulled in behind. Jerman and Dewey got out and headed to the car.

Jaime was kicking the tire and cursing.

"That ain't gonna help, Jaime. Open the trunk. Let's get this done before a cop stops and gives us trouble."

Jaime gave Jerman a cold stare. "You don't give me orders, punk. You go and get me the spare." He punched the fob and the trunk flipped open."

Jerman put his hand inside his shirt. "I was not giving you orders, but I might, or I just shoot your ass. I don't change tires."

Dewey decided he didn't want to be in another gunfight.

"You are gonna help." Jaime pointed at Dewey.

"You said it yourself, Jaime. I drive. Don't do tires, either. I'll be in the truck when you guys are ready to go." He gave him the finger, turned, and walked back to the truck.

He sat in the truck and watched Jaime and the other man fiddle with the spare. Jerman stood and watched. It was obvious that Jerman, as Miguel's nephew, was in charge.

Dewey grabbed his bottle of Red Bull and took a swig. Might as well relax and wait for the car to be drivable again.

He didn't have a lot of time to relax before he heard sirens. The flashers of a cop car appeared in his rearview mirror. *Shit! Cops! Maybe they're just after a speeder. Couldn't be after us, could they?* He started the truck just in case.

Then another cop car appeared on the other side of the Interstate heading his way, lights flashing and sirens blaring. The passenger side door banged open and Jerman jumped in.

"Move it. Somehow they ID'd us."

Dewey didn't need Jerman's advice. He'd accelerated and guided the truck back on the road.

"We sure as hell can't outrun the cops in this thing." Dewey's fingers gripped the steering wheel so hard they turned white. Sweat furrowed down his back.

"Go on this road at a safe speed. About ten miles ahead I know a place where we can hide for a while. Had a girlfriend up here a couple years back. Her folks have a farm there. Big barn we can use."

Dewey set the cruise at sixty-five.

Jerman pointed to an exit for Slade, Missouri. "Turn

here. Go left."

They turned onto two-lane Highway J. About a mile and a half further Jerman gestured. "Here. Turn right."

It would only qualify as little more than a dirt path. The truck lurched down the lane threatening to tip over a couple of times from deep potholes. Less than a half mile in, they came to a farmhouse with a huge barn facing it.

"Park in front of the barn. I'll go see if they're home. Wait here." Jerman got out and sauntered over to the house. He climbed the stairs to the porch and knocked on the door. No answer. He knocked again. Nothing. He peeked into the front window shading his eyes.

Finally, he walked back and opened the truck's door. He didn't get in.

"I'm gonna see if the barn door is unlocked and you can pull the truck inside."

He closed the door and walked up a small incline to the barn. He took a look and gave Dewey a thumb's up. He shoved one side of the double doors to the right and did the same with the left one. They screeched loudly.

Dewey pulled the truck inside and parked toward the back up against a pile of hay bales. He got out and walked back to Jerman. The floor of the barn covered with hay smelled musty.

"Gimme the keys." Jerman held out his hands and Dewey dropped the key.

"You think I'm gonna take the truck and leave you here?" Dewey smirked.

"Nope, not if I got the key. I don't know you so I'm being cautious."

"Well, it would be really stupid of me to take off and leave Miguel's nephew to answer to the cops, wouldn't it?"

"True but that is again something I don't know about you. You could be stupid. We will wait here. If these people show up, we'll get something to eat. If they don't, we might break in and get something anyway."

"I am kind a hungry," Dewey replied.

****

A Missouri State Police car appeared in Chase's rearview mirror, lights flashing and sirens blaring. Chase had stopped far enough away from the Camaro so the cop had plenty of room to pull in front of him. He skidded to a stop about three car lengths behind the Camaro with his car sideways on the road blocking northbound traffic.

Another police car approached from the opposite side of the highway and slid to a stop on the median. The first officer opened his door and aimed a weapon at the Camaro.

Jaime and the other man hunkered down in the ditch beside the road. They climbed up the embankment, opened the back door of the car and removed rifles from the back seat.

Traffic slowed and then stopped when they saw a police car blocking the highway and a confrontation about to take place.

The Washburn's truck suddenly took off. Chase couldn't let them get away and the police had no reason to stop them right now. He gunned the engine and followed the truck blasting past the scene hoping no bullets from either side came his way.

So far it seems to be a Mexican standoff. Oops, probably politically incorrect. But actually, it's true.

Washburn didn't speed. The truck continued at a reasonable sixty-five mph. Not hard to keep sight of.

Chase heard no gunfire behind him so maybe Jaime and the other guy surrendered. Not his worry. And there were only two guys left to deal with.

A few miles from the Camaro, the truck turned onto a rural highway toward Shade, Missouri. Chase followed a good distance behind. After another mile or so, Washburn turned down a dirt road.

Chase drove on past the road, stopping next to a cornfield. His car would be hidden from wherever Washburn stopped. He got out, grabbed his backpack, and trotted along the field back toward the path he'd seen Washburn enter.

Peering around the edge of the field he watched the truck's passenger exit and walk up on the porch of an old farmhouse. The man returned to the truck after a few minutes when he apparently found no one home.

Chase drew his EMP and ducked into the second row of corn. He crouched and swam through the field toward the old red barn towering above the corn. He was glad he wore his light brown Khakis and matching shirt. He'd pretty much blend in with the field.

The atmosphere inside the rows seemed like a sauna. Thankfully he could still see the dirt path off to his right. Otherwise everywhere he looked stalks of corn waved in the breeze. He'd even heard of farmers getting lost in a cornfield where you couldn't see any way out. An almost constant stream of bugs flew into his face.

As he neared the barn, he heard Washburn and the other man talking but he couldn't make out what they were saying. A loud squeak of something heavy moving startled him. He moved closer. Through the stalks he saw the wheels of the truck in front of the barn and a man's legs standing in back.

The truck rolled into the barn and then a second squeak turned out to be Washburn closing the barn doors. Soon Washburn's legs met the others.

Just as Chase prepared to jump out of the field to get the drop on the two, another truck bounced up the path. Nuts! Nothing Chase could do but wait. Could be additional gunmen.

A 1980s F-150 came into view but Chase couldn't make out the driver. It pulled up in front of the barn and stopped. Two doors clanged shut.

I don't think Washburn could've called in reinforcements so quickly. This must be whoever owns the farm. Still could be trouble though.

The old military saying came to mind. Whatever could go wrong, will.

Chapter 37

An old faded blue F-150 rolled up the path toward Jerman and Dewey. When it stopped in front of the house two people got out. The passenger stood looking over the bed of the truck. She had long, stringy white hair and square glasses that reflected sunlight. Her face, a mass of wrinkles, didn't have a happy look.

The man at the driver's door, stooped over a bit, wore an untucked, green, and white checkered shirt and jeans with a belt barely visible underneath a huge belly. Clear blue eyes stared at Jerman.

"Thought you weren't supposed to come back here, ever, Herman." The rough, gravelly voice belied years of smoking.

"Now don't be like that, John. I was in the neighborhood and wanted to say hi." Jerman extended his hand and walked over to the man.

"You're not welcome. Just hightail it on outta here. Take your friend with you." He didn't shake Jerman's hand.

"Don't be like that, John. I remember you and Rose as very nice and hospitable people. We've been traveling a long way and just wanted to stop somewhere to rest. Couldn't we just stay in the barn for a while? We'd be no bother."

"You'll be less of a bother by movin' on. Last time you were here I told you it would be the last time. That hasn't changed."

He started to turn away and Jerman grabbed his arm in a vice-like grip.

"I'm afraid we have no choice. We are staying for a while. You need to get used to that."

John tried to jerk his arm away and couldn't. He swung a feeble punch and missed. "Let me go." Jerman just laughed.

His wife screamed and ran toward the house. Jerman pulled his Glock and fired into the air. Rose froze.

"Rose, stop. We won't hurt you, but you need to do as I say, or maybe John gets hurt. Neither of us wants that."

Rose stood shaking. "What do you want from us?"

"Before we were willing to stay in the barn for a bit. Now, I think we will all go in the house. Maybe you can fix us something to eat. We'll have a nice breakfast. Okay?"

Rose slowly nodded her head. "Let him go."

Jerman released John's arm and he hobbled over to Rose and put his arm around her. They walked up the steps and onto the porch. John took one last look at Jerman and shook his head. He unlocked the door and they entered.

****

Chase peered through the cornstalks. The old woman ran toward the house. Chase flinched when he heard a gunshot. The partner had fired into the air as he talked to the old man.

Chase flipped off the safety on his EMP and aimed it at the Hispanic man. He couldn't get a clear shot because the truck blocked his view, complicated by the darkness of early morning. If he had to confront them, he'd have to move to improve his line of sight.

Then the man lowered his weapon and released the old man. They talked and he watched as Washburn and the others entered the house. The older couple didn't look pleased with their visitors. Washburn's partner shoved the old man up the stairs before they went in. The guy didn't look happy that the two guys had showed up.

Chase hunched over and ran to the side of the old truck. The four people disappeared deeper inside the house. He mounted the stairs, hoping the porch was solid enough not to make any loud noise. So far, so good. He leaned against the front door listening for movement inside. Nothing.

Chase regretted that apparently innocent people had become involved. Dealing with a hostage situation was the last thing he needed. No matter. He couldn't let Dewey get away. And he wouldn't.

****

Dewey and Jerman herded John and Rose into the kitchen. Dewey took a chair at the small round table adjacent to the kitchen. Old yellow appliances dating to perhaps the 70s were clean and shining brightly. He rested his arms on the Formica top.

Jerman gestured to one of the remaining three empty kitchen chairs. "John, why don't you sit and keep Dewey company while Rose fixes us something to eat?"

John sat next to Dewey and Jerman took the chair opposite John. He laid the Glock on the table and sat back.

"What you going to make for us, Rose?" Jerman had a jagged smile on his face.

"I don't know. We haven't gotten to the store yet, so I don't know what I have. Wait." She opened the refrigerator door. "How about eggs? I could fix an omelet."

"Sounds good to me. How 'bout you, Dewey?"

"I like omelets. That'll do fine."

Rose removed an egg carton from the fridge and placed it on the counter. She then gathered some cheese, bell peppers, and mushrooms. Jerman leaned back in his chair and tapped the table in front of him.

"How is Carolyn?" He smiled.

"She's doing fine. In college and away from you." John's fist clenched and his jaw tightened.

"Don't be like that. I liked her. She was nice and a spitfire."

"We aren't going to talk about her. She told me how you treated her. Striking her. If I was anywhere near my shotgun, you'd be full of buckshot."

"She seemed to like me when I was here. My life was messed up some then, but I'm fine now."

"Don't sound like it. You're here looking to hide for some reason. We don't wish to be involved in whatever you're in to. Please leave."

"Not gonna happen right now."

They watched Rose prepare breakfast.

A few minutes later, Rose served the eggs and poured coffee into cups for each. She returned to the counter and started to fix a plate for herself.

"Rose, come and sit at the table with us. You are being inhospitable eating over there." Jerman patted the chair next to him.

Rose looked at the chair and then at John. He nodded and she moved her plate and cup to the table. She pulled the chair back and sat, trying to stay as far away from Jerman as possible.

"I just want you to know that if John was near his shotgun, I'd be handin' him some shells." Rose stared daggers at Jerman.

Jerman looked at Rose for a few seconds and burst out laughing. "I like you, Rose. You are a no-nonsense lady. You speak to me disrespectfully even though you know I could put a bullet in your head.

"You got guts. I give you much credit. But I wouldn't do anything rash if I were you." He picked up his Glock and pointed it at Rose. "I will not hesitate to shoot you or John if you don't do as I say. Are we clear?"

John and Rose nodded. Dewey sat eating his omelet, his face showing no expression.

"Now here's what we will do. Dewey and I will stay here for a day or so. You will feed us and then we will go. If you cooperate, we'll let you live. Pretty simple. Understand?"

They glanced at each other and nodded.

"Okay, we're clear on that. Now, where is this famous shotgun, John?"

"Hall closet, top shelf." He pointed to the hall.

Jerman got up, picked up his pistol and went to the closet. He pulled out the rifle and checked to ensure it wasn't loaded, returned to the kitchen, then handed it to Dewey.

"Take care of this. Okay, I also want your cell phones please." Jerman held out a hand.

John pulled an iPhone from his pocket and placed it on the table. Jerman looked at Rose.

"I don't have one." She folded her arms across her chest.

"A landline? I think I remember you have one of those?"

Roses eyes widened. "Uh, yes. In the living room."

Jerman went around the corner and came back with a phone trailing a frayed cord.

"Now we're good." He dropped the phone into a garbage container by the back door. "Let's pretend we're just one big happy family."

****

Chase crept down the front steps and rounded the corner of the house. He kept close to the house in the shade. He stopped and listened. Muffled voices came from the back. He moved closer till he came to a window.

One of the men asked for breakfast. Hunkered down under the window, Chase couldn't risk a look to see where everyone was, and he needed to find out. About twenty-five yards behind the house a grove of tall pin oaks afforded a good view of the window. If he could get to those trees he could climb up and see inside.

Chase headed back to the cornfield where he could stay out of view and come close to the trees. The field wound around the back allowing him to reach the trees from the edge and only risk being seen for few feet.

Ten minutes later he squatted between two giant cornstalks only ten feet or so from an oak probably forty feet high with branches full of leaves that'd keep him hidden. He released a breath and took off for the tree. He quickly climbed into the foliage and mounted a limb with a perfect view of the kitchen. He laid flat on the limb.

Inside three men sat at a table, the older gentleman, Dewey, and the Hispanic man. The woman worked at a stove preparing food. Through his binoculars Washburn sat facing him through the window, the Hispanic seated on the right side and the old man on the left. The woman began serving food to the men and eventually sat down opposite Dewey.

The Hispanic man placed a pistol on the table and began talking. Chase couldn't hear what he said but obviously instructions were being issued. He didn't have his rifle with him so taking the two men out wasn't a viable option with just a handgun. He needed to find an opportunity and act.

The four talked for a bit and then suddenly the Hispanic man pointed the gun at the old woman. Chase reached for his EMP and aimed at the man. He didn't want to fire and reveal his position but if he was going to shoot the woman, he had no choice.

The man finally lowered the gun and they resumed talking. He stood and walked into the hallway and returned with a rifle that he handed over to Washburn. Then he opened his hand and said something to the old man.

The old man pulled his phone out of his pocket and handed it to the man. He asked another question, got up and left. He carried an old black phone with a cord dangling from it when he returned. No phone service for the pair.

It seemed that Dewey and his partner were going to make the couple fix meals and become servants for them. Hopefully that would keep them safe until Chase could figure out a way to protect them.

The truck the men had escaped in now sat in the barn. Chase decided to try to get to it and disable it so Washburn would have no way to escape. He climbed down and hurried back into the field.

A few minutes later he reached the barn door. He tried moving it and a loud squeak halted him. It was loud enough to be heard from inside if he pushed the doors open. Maybe there's another way in. Chase walked around the side of the barn and saw no windows or doors. He continued around the back to the other side of the barn where he found a door.

It was unlocked and he slipped inside. In the darkness he could make out the white truck and he moved to the driver's side. He gently opened the door and searched for the hood release. None.

At the front of the truck, he found the latch and lifted the hood. The connection for the fuel pump gas intake had a small hose that was easy to remove. He laid it on the motor head and closed the hood as quietly as he could. That truck would not move until the hose was reconnected. Good.

Now to disable those two guys.

Chapter 38

Jerman finished his eggs and reached for his coffee as his phone buzzed.

"*Hola, Tio.*" He wiped a crumb from his mustache.

"Where are you, Jerman?" Miguel sounded upset.

"We are in backwater Missouri. Had to find a place to lay low for a bit."

"How is my truck? Jaime and Andoval got stopped by the cops. What happened?"

"I don't know. They had a flat and all of a sudden cops showed up. Had them pinned down. We took off. No choice. They didn't chase us. Is Jaime all right?"

"Stupid idiots tried to shoot it out. Jaime is dead and Andoval is in the hospital. Probably won't make it. Glad you left."

"No way we were going to stay."

"This is nuts. Are you going to be able to make it here okay?"

"We're about six hours away. We will stay here for a couple of hours to allow more traffic on the road to blend in better. I'll take the lettering strip off the truck's door to disguise it more."

"I am counting on you, Jerman. This is my biggest shipment ever, and I can't afford to lose it."

"You know you can count on me. I will get it there."

"Make sure you do. Is Dewey there?"

"Yes."

"Are you on speaker?"

"No."

"It would be good to not have to deal with him anymore. Get rid of him on the way." Miguel hung up.

Dewey looked up from his breakfast. "How's Miguel? What happened after we left?"

"Jaime and Andoval tried to escape and got into a gunfight with the cops. He's dead and Andoval's probably not gonna to make it."

"Good thing we left. Miguel okay with what we did?"

"Sure. He's obsessing about us getting back. Got a bundle of money riding on this one. We better not screw it up."

"Agreed."

Rose and John sat wide-eyed listening to the two men talk. Jerman got up and went to the back door.

"I'm going to take the lettering off the truck. Be back in a minute." He left.

Jerman lit a cigarette and walked down the porch steps. The place hadn't changed at all since he'd been here, what was it? Had to be four years at least. He dated Carolyn for almost two years before she broke it off when she went to finish her degree at the university. He was tired of her anyway.

The early sun began to peek through the horizon. Jerman glanced at his watch. Just before five. He figured they'd wait till about seven and try to get lost in the early morning traffic. He took a deep drag and slowly let the smoke trickle out of his nose. Too bad about the old couple. Can't have any witnesses left.

The barn doors squeaked loudly as he entered the darkened interior. He approached the truck and stopped.

A strong gasoline smell surrounded the vehicle. He grabbed his cigarette and searched for a place to put it out. A hot ash fell and landed on the hay-covered floor. As he tapped the floor to put it out, sparks spread to pooling gasoline and flames burst out from under the truck.

He tried to locate something to beat out the worst of the fire before it expanded into a full-blown blaze. Stripping off his shirt he slashed at the growing mass. It only intensified. The more he swung, the more it spread. Soon the middle of the barn was a pit of burning flames.

He dropped his shirt as it too had caught the flames. He bolted for the doors. The ammunition in the truck caught fire and exploded, and the blast hurled Jerman into the wall.

Lying on his side, he watched through a huge gash in the side of the van as a pile of Miguel's packages engulfed in flames slowly disappeared. His mind began envisioning the aftermath of this disaster. Thoughts whirled in his head. Thoughts of how Miguel would react when he found out his shipment burned. Thoughts about the lack of pain he should be feeling as he noticed the bloody tines of a pitchfork protruding from his chest.

His last conscious thought questioned how in the world had he missed seeing that tool when he'd looked around inside.

****

Chase watched Jerman enter the barn. He moved from the rows of corn to the side door he'd entered earlier. Now would be a good time to take one of these guys out. He drew his knife and slipped inside.

The man stood to the front of the truck and a puff of smoke lifted above his head. He swung a piece of cloth

173

trying to snuff out flames as they shot up around him. Then Chase noticed a strong smell of gasoline. Uh oh. The hose must have slipped off the motor mount spilling gas onto the floor.

The flames began to overcome the man and Chase sprinted for the door. He'd just left the barn when it erupted in an explosion that shook the ground, knocking him to the ground. Something heavy crashed into wall, and flames shot out the opening. It wouldn't take long before the barn would be engulfed.

Chase needed to get to the side of the house before Washburn came out. He ducked back into the corn and made his way again to where he could get a view of the front of the house. Sure enough, Washburn sped out the front door and down the steps, sliding to a stop at the hood of the old pickup.

Chase drew his EMP and darted out of the stalks.

"Hold it right there, Washburn!"

Dewey turned and blinked his eyes. He swiveled his head from the barn to Anderson and back, like he couldn't figure out which to concentrate on.

John burst out of the house and stopped at the stairs. He stared at the barn now fully engulfed in flames. Rose joined him and grabbed his hand. John turned and looked into her tear-filled eyes. He threw his arm around her shoulders and mouthed the words, "It's okay, my love."

"Get back in the house." Chase yelled at the couple.

Before anyone could react, Washburn jumped up the steps and grabbed Rose. He drew his pistol and snapped a quick shot at Chase, missing him as he retreated into the corn stalks. With the barn to his left, he figured Washburn would fire into the field thinking that's the way Chase would go, so he went right deeper into the field. Bullets penetrated the rows but came nowhere near him.

Washburn guessed Anderson would head toward the barn. He emptied his magazine more to give himself some time than thinking he could hit him. He inserted another.

And how in the world did Anderson show up here? No way could he have found him here. Dewey didn't even know where Jerman had been heading after escaping the cops.

Rose still held John's hand as he tried to pry Washburn's hand from Rose. Washburn knocked John's hand away and herded the couple into the house.

"Do you have a basement?" Dewey asked John.

"Yes, through the kitchen. Door next to the fridge."

"Let's go then." He motioned with his gun, and they shuffled into the kitchen.

At the basement door, Dewey opened it and pointed to the steps.

"John, is there another way out of the basement?"

"No."

"Hand the me the key that locks this door." He held out his hand.

John pulled a set of keys from his pocket and pointed to one. "This one locks the door."

Dewey grabbed the keys and ushered John and Rose down the stairs. He locked the door and went to the kitchen window facing the field.

He stood to the side and allowed one eye to scan the cornfield. He thought he could locate Anderson by finding where the top of the stalks moved. That proved useless as a brisk wind blew across the rows.

At the side window a giant ball of flames towered over the barn. The inferno would certainly draw the attention of neighbors and the fire department would be here soon.

The keys in his hand would start the truck. *Best for me to leave. No way to save Miguel's shipment. He's gonna be pissed. And where's Jerman?*

He grabbed his phone and punched Miguel's number.

"Miguel, we got big trouble."

"What now?"

"Hate to tell you but your shipment is now burning up. I can't find Jerman. He might be dead."

"How did that happen? You are dead. And any family you got left is dead!"

"Wasn't my fault. This guy Anderson, I told you about. He's here. Don't know how he got on to us, but he burned the truck in a barn here. I'm leaving, heading back to Chicago."

"No! You find my nephew. Don't come back here alone. Find him. Kill Anderson or don't show up in Chicago. You will need a coffin." The line went dead.

Dewey stared at the phone. *How am I gonna take on Anderson? The guy's creepy. Like a ghost. Nope. I gotta go.* He headed to the front door. At the window he searched the area around the truck. Nothing.

He went outside, crouching on the porch. Looked clear. He jumped down off the porch and opened the truck's door. Climbing in he searched the keyring for the right key and found it. He started the engine, shoved the gear into drive and stomped on the accelerator.

The vehicle jerked and scattered gravel as he sped down the path between rows of corn. Miguel's phone burst apart as he tossed it out the window. He threw his own phone on the passenger seat.

Time to become a new man. Dewey Washburn has disappeared.

****

The early morning sun had begun to warm up the field. Sweat burned his eyes as Chase wove through the stalks. He'd angled back toward the rear of the house and felt he was just a few rows from the grassy area between the house and the corn.

Along the way a startled family of skunks crossed in front of him. He'd held his breath hoping they would shuffle away rather than try to spray him. She stared at him and with a nose wiggle, momma skunk decided to retreat from danger and pushed her three youngsters ahead of her, waddling away from Chase.

He finally reached the edge of the field and could see the house not far away. Taking a chance that Washburn wasn't in the kitchen, he scooted up to the back of the home. A breeze cooled him off as he duck-walked around the corner to the left side of the house. He eased up to the edge of the porch and poked his head around the side.

Then he heard a voice coming from behind him. He backtracked to a side window and put his ear to the siding. Someone was speaking but he couldn't make out what was being said. He rose up and peered into the window. He thought he saw Washburn standing next to the refrigerator. The man's feet and his elbow were all Chase could see.

Suddenly Washburn ran out of the kitchen heading

for the front door. No sign of the old man or woman. Chase heard Washburn open the front door and go out on the porch. Chase would be an easy target in the open, squatting next to the house. Diving on the ground he lay as flat as he could and aimed his EMP at the corner where Washburn would be if he looked for Chase.

Other than the popping and crackling of the fire at the barn the only noise came from three crows cawing at each other as they waddled on the ground near the field.

A truck started up and Chase heard the tires slip on the gravel as it tried to get traction. He got up and sprinted to the front of the house. The blue pickup sped by, and Chase took aim. A phone flew out of the truck's window as Chase fired three times at the man inside.

For a moment Chase thought he'd missed, but then the truck veered to the right, plowing through several rows of corn. He jogged toward the downed stalks and followed them to the stalled vehicle. He crept up to the window and looked inside.

Washburn, draped across the steering wheel, made no sound. Still aiming his EMP at the driver, Chase carefully pulled him back by his shirt. Washburn sprawled in the seat and turned his head toward Chase. Blood pooled down his neck and shoulder.

He swallowed and gazed at Chase. "How…?"

His eyes blinked and deep in his throat a gurgle erupted, then he collapsed onto the passenger seat. He wouldn't be coming after Chase anymore. The war finally ended.

****

An hour and a half after Dewey's call, Miguel smacked his desktop so hard his hand went numb. For the third time in the last hour Jerman failed to answer his call.

"Where is he?" He tried once more.

"Answer me!" Nothing.

He tried Dewey's phone again.

"Hello?" The voice wasn't Dewey's

"Dewey?"

"Who is this?" a gruff voice asked.

"I'm trying to reach Dewey Washburn. He's a friend. Who's this?"

"This is the police. How do you know Mr. Washburn?"

"He's a business acquaintance. Why do you have his phone?"

"We are conducting an investigation. Can I have your name please?"

Miguel hung up. Police? An investigation? Shit!

"Shonte? Git in here."

Shonte Williams hurried inside the office. "Yeah, boss?"

"I can't get Jerman or Dewey on the phone. And the cops have Dewey's cell. They said they're investigating. Find out what's going on? Something happened to my shipment, we got big trouble."

"Right on it." He ran out the door. Miguel stood so fast his chair shot back into the file cabinet.

****

Fifteen minutes later, Shonte knocked on Miguel's door and opened it.

"Not good news. Seems that a barn in Missouri burned up with a truck inside. They recovered a body and are trying to identify it."

"Crap! Jerman or Dewey."

"Sorry, boss. It had to be Jerman because they also found Dewey. He got shot. Was some kind of hostage thing they think. Some dude from Louisiana rescued the old couple who owned the farm. Dewey's dead. Not a lot of details being released."

"Louisiana? Was that the guy Dewey was telling me about? He and his brother went down there to settle a score and Drew got killed. That the same guy?"

"Didn't give out the guy's name. I'll try to get more from the Internet."

"Get me a hammer."

When Shonte returned Miguel grabbed the hammer, placed the cell on his desk, and smashed it.

"Clean that up and find out what's going on. Call me on my main number. I'm gonna go for a walk. Think this thing through."

Miguel grabbed a pack of cigarettes from his desk drawer, letting loose a string of profanity. He slammed the office door so hard the walls shook.

Chapter 39

Chris Martinez sat on a warehouse bench and rubbed the stubble of his beard. He hated waiting. He felt the patience he lacked he compensated with perseverance. Never mind the fact that he'd washed out of Navy Seal training due to that absence of patience. Surely the remainder of the squad would show up soon.

Chris' friend Shonte stood next to a black SUV parked in front of the office. It sparkled under the fluorescent lights. Five men would fit comfortably in it, as would their gear.

Two men sat across from him on a separate hard wooden bench. All heavily armed and dressed in black jeans and shirts. Chris carried the knife he had swiped from the Seal storehouse on his belt along with a filled canteen. His backpack contained a Glock 22, extra ammo, his AK-47, night vision goggles, and a generous supply of protein bars.

He knew the men as Carlos and Joe, but not he suspected their real names. They spoke in Spanish exclusively. Chris didn't care. His fluency in Spanish remained a secret. He hadn't let on that he understood everything they said. He used the alias, Fred.

Finally, the rest of the crew arrived. Tomas and Alfredo halted beside the others and nodded when Shonte introduced them. All the men except for Shonte stood six feet tall and only one was chunky. Shonte then introduced Miguel, the shortest man in the room.

"Gentlemen this is a very important task I'm asking you to tackle. Two days ago, my nephew was killed, and I lost my shipment. You're going to Louisiana to recover that shipment if it's there.

"You're being paid well, and I expect nothing but complete success. Shonte has given you the details. Fred is in charge. Follow his direction. No one is to escape. I want Anderson dead. Bring pictures. Any questions?"

No one spoke.

"Fred, you want to say anything?"

"Only that we'll take turns driving. It's going to be eighteen hours so get some rest during the drive if you can. Stow your gear in the back.

"If we get stopped for any reason, I do the talking. No one else. When we stop for meals stick to yourself, do nothing that will make us stand out. Everyone have a valid driver's license?"

All nodded except for the chunky guy, Tomas.

"Okay, Tomas, you drive first. It's one a.m. so you take the first three hours. I'll ride shotgun. GPS has our route calculated so just follow what it says. When we get there, I'll issue instructions for the attack. Let's go."

****

Chase sat at the breakfast table staring at a huge plate of pancakes next to an equally huge plate of scrambled eggs, sweet honey ham and sugared hush puppies. Char and Lettie handed orange juice glasses and coffee cups to Beau and Chase. The women had insisted on preparing a celebration now that he was back and safe.

"Lettie, I noticed I only received one of those awesome hush puppies of yours. Did you forget to give me a full share?" Beau took the coffee and smiled at Lettie.

"That is your full share 'cording to your Doc." She slapped him on the shoulder. "I already overdid it with your pancake."

"Again, that is singular, as in only one." He frowned. "How am I supposed to get through the day on this piddlin' amount?"

"Due to that amount, you still have a chance to make it through the day. You should thank me, but I know ya won't." She sat next to Chase.

"I think I'm going to have to spend the entire morning walking off my breakfast. This is a feast. Thank you, ladies." Chase lifted his orange juice glass in a toast.

The night before, Chase had related his encounter and filled his family in on all the details of his adventure with Washburn and the drug runners. The FBI, Missouri State Police, and local Sheriff had questioned Chase for five hours. Finally satisfied they released him to return home with the stipulation that he would come back should they need additional information.

"Lettie, would you share a prayer of thanks for us?" Beau nodded and lowered his head.

"Dear Father, thank you for answering our prayers for Chase and bringing him home. Please forgive Mr. Beau as he reaches for more of those hush puppies. Bless this food we are about to receive. Amen.

Beau released the third hush puppy back onto the plate and smiled. "Caught me." He took a bite of one of the newly swiped treats. "Yummy."

"We're so glad everything turned out okay. We were worried sick that something would happen." Char swiped a tear away.

"Fortunately, John and Rose, the couple who own the farm, were able to confirm my story. And the fact that the FBI as well as the Louisiana Parrish Sheriff had a warrant for Washburn's arrest concerning the mess he caused here, made it easy to see the whole story. And Lettie, there's some unfinished business we need to take care of."

"Unfinished business? What's that?" She took a sip of juice.

"How about that movie and a burger tonight?"

"Tonight? Aren't you just wantin' to relax after your ordeal? We can always go to a movie."

"Nope. I think a movie and a burger with a pretty woman is just the thing to relax me." He held up both hands. "Not a date you understand. Just a nice evening for relaxation."

Char and Beau exchanged wide smiles.

"Well, I guess if it helps you relax, how can I say no?" Lettie's face had taken on a pinkish tone.

Promptly at 5:30 Chase pulled the Mercury around to the back door and climbed the steps. A steady rain brought out the fresh smell of damp earth. He'd put on his best Khaki dress slacks and a light blue button-pocket, short-sleeved, shirt for his non-date. Although it did kind of seem like a date. He opened his umbrella.

As he reached for the doorknob, it opened. Lettie, dressed in an ankle-length, navy dress with white piping around the collar and down the front, sashayed out and closed the door.

"I hate to keep anyone waiting. 'Specially since I'm goin' to a movie."

"Don't you look nice. Guys are gonna be real

jealous of me, escorting such a beautiful Lady."

"Why thank you, kind sir. You look nice yourself. Maybe the guys aren't the only ones being jealous."

They waved at Char and Beau hovering at the kitchen window, all smiles, and headed to Joe's Cajun Burgers 'N Such.

****

Joe's place bustled with activity. Chase breathed a sigh of relief when Lettie suggested they eat on the patio. The light rain had no strong winds to push it under the tin roofed canopy and the night temperature was a pleasant seventy-two degrees. Only three other couples occupied tables when they entered, and the lowered noise volume allowed them to converse without having to yell.

After ordering iced tea, they asked for time to look over the menu.

"I like this place a lot. Have you been here often?" Lettie tucked a loose curl behind her ear.

"A couple of times. If I'd known this patio was here, I would have come here a lot more. I'm not one for much noise and commotion."

"Me, too. Give me a quiet place every time."

The waitress brought their drinks and stood waiting for their order.

"I'll have the Cajun burger and cheese fries, please." She took a sip of tea.

"Sounds good to me. Same."

"Been wonderin' somethin' about you, Chase?"

"Uh oh." He smiled.

"No. Nothin' bad. Just that Chase is such an unusual name. Is it given or a nickname?"

"Whew. I thought you were going to ask a tough

question. It's actually my first name. Mom and Dad had an agreement that he would pick a boy's name and she would pick a girl's name. Dad named me Chase because that's what he had to do to, as he put it, corral my mom. Middle name is Stuart, Mom's maiden name."

"What does your dad do?"

"He was an engineer. Died nine years ago. Heart. Mom died three years ago from cancer."

"I'm so sorry. Any siblings?"

"Nope, I was an only. Was a difficult birth and she wasn't able to have any more children."

"Leave it to me to drag up unhappiness."

"No, not a big deal. Frankly, I was relieved when my mom passed. She was in so much pain and discomfort, I was happy that it went away. At that point death was welcome for both of us. She fought as long as she could."

"I understand. One day someone will find a cure for cancer, and we'll all be the better."

"I believe that."

"What are you interested in doing? I mean as far as work?"

"With my military background my skills are limited for civilian professions. I only have two years of college so whatever I decide will require additional education. Maybe something in law enforcement."

"Why not education? I think you'd make a great teacher."

"Hadn't given that any thought at all." He sat for a minute. "I'll look into that. Thanks for the suggestion."

Their meal came and they dug in. Chase enjoyed being with Lettie. She was kind, smart and seemingly uncomplicated. A trait he greatly admired. His Lily had been the same. Easy to see how those two were like sisters. They were wrestling with having dessert when Chase's cell buzzed.

"Hello, Beau. You checking up on us?" He grinned at Lettie.

"You need to come back, Chase. Char and I are in the safe room. We have armed men swarming the property. I've called the police."

"How many men?"

"Far as I can tell, five maybe six. Armed with rifles. We're okay for now. Your gate stopped them. I think their car got stuck in the mud trying to get around the gate. The alarm beeped loudly, and I saw them walking down the drive. We skittered to the safe room. Good thing it's in the back of the house."

"Stay there and don't make any noise."

"We're both armed and if they breach the door some of them are not going to remain healthy."

"Don't try to be a hero. Last resort is to fight. I'm on my way."

He hung up.

"What's happening?" Lettie grabbed his arm.

"Some armed men at the house. I want you to take a cab to the Sheriff's office. They've already been called but make sure they know what's going on. It'll be the safest place for you."

"Okay. What about you?"

"We're being attacked again and I'm going to help end it. It's what I know how to do. Promise me you'll go to the sheriff. I don't want to worry about you getting hurt."

"I will. Be careful. I know that's a cliché, but it applies."

Lettie left and Chase paid the bill. He jogged to the

car and raced back home. *What a time to be in my civies. Got to try to get to the shack where my gear is.*

Chase felt the rush of adrenaline he'd experienced on many overseas missions. This one though, was different. His family facing danger and his absence worried him.

He pushed the old Mercury as much as he could and still avoid an accident. The men who showed up tonight didn't have a clue that someone like him now had them as targets. He had to protect Beau and Char. Someone would pay a price. A very severe price indeed.

Chapter 40

The GPS announced that they had reached their destination. Carlos turned into the driveway and stopped at the security gate. The wipers cleared the rain, showing a solid metal post with a code box at driver's height next to the road. The box was set into a frame designed to look like a small house with a roof protecting the keyboard.

"See if you can get that thing to work, Carlos." Chris Martinez sat in the seat behind the driver.

Carlos muttered something and got out. He pushed the buttons and jimmied the gate. He returned to the SUV and climbed in.

"Solid. Gonna need a tank to crash through that." He wiped the rain out of his eyes.

"Can we get around the gate?"

"Your guess is as good as mine. Water on both sides of it filling the shoulder. This has four-wheel drive. We could try."

"Do it."

Carlos backed up and eased into the side of the driveway. The car leaned to the left and all five occupants leaned to the right by instinct. The car finally settled into a track in the water.

Carlos maneuvered forward and by the time they had pulled even with the gate, the SUV had completely sunk into the mud. Shifting from forward to back several times resulted in making the car stuck so badly it hardly moved.

"Crap! Okay everybody out and push. Carlos try steering us back to the driveway." Chris crawled out and the four men waded into the water.

They heaved and grunted for a good five minutes in waist-deep water, making little or no headway. The muddy bottom threatened to pull their boots off their feet. It quickly became clear the SUV was immobile.

"All right, listen up. We'll hike in from here. Everyone grab your gear. Test your comms." Chris tapped his earbuds. "Testing, one here."

All answered good to go.

"Tomas, you and Carlos take positions at the cabin on stilts in the back. If you see movement let me know. Alfredo, you and me, we'll take the house. Joe, you stay here and watch for anybody who shows up. They have a Mercury and a Hummer. When we're done, we'll take the Hummer. I'll bet it'll get through that gate.

"Anybody but the Anderson guy we take as a hostage to flush him out. Don't kill them and try not to hurt them. Everybody good?"

They pulled each other out of the ditch and trudged down the drive, rifles at the ready. They were four armed men with substantial firepower. Should be enough for a bunch of civilians.

The rain continued to fall. Two powerful lights over the garage illuminated the back of the mansion. So much for his night vision goggles. Chris saw no sign of activity. Tomas and Carlos crept toward the stilted house. They fanned out each taking a side of the gravel path. Chris and Joe watched till they crouched down in the grass to wait.

Chris tried the back door. Locked. He took out a

lock pick and they were inside in less than a minute. They stopped, listening. Music came from somewhere off to the right. Down a hall past the dining room Chris stepped to the left side of a door, Joe took the right. He nodded and Joe entered the room sweeping his rifle. Chris followed. No one there. Living room and the TV was on.

They methodically checked every room in the house. It was empty.

"Where they at? We'll wait. And why's the TV on?"

"I'm hungry. I'll check the kitchen." Joe lowered his rifle and walked back down the hall.

Chris tapped his comm. "House is empty. Tomas check the garage. Make sure no one is hiding there."

A few minutes later he reported.

"Garage is clear. The hummer is here but the other car is gone."

"Okay return to your position. We wait."

"I noticed a door around the back. Looks like it could lead to a basement. It's shut tight. Tried to open it, but no dice. Maybe they're hiding there."

"Did you hear anything inside?"

"All quiet."

Chris joined Joe in the kitchen. "Something ain't right. Look at the table. Dishes set and some food still on the plates. Looks like someone left quick. Joe, see if you can find a basement."

"Usually, you can get to the basement from the kitchen. Only door here is the pantry and it doesn't seem like there'd be any way to get to a basement from there. I think we opened every door in the house already." Joe munched on a chicken leg he'd found in the fridge.

"I'm going to check that door outside. Could be a

place to hide." Chris left the kitchen and crossed the porch. He could see the door Tomas had spotted. He walked up and tried the handle. With both hands he tugged on the door again. No luck. He put his ear to the door and heard nothing.

He pounded on the door. "Anybody in there?"

Silence.

"If you don't answer, I'm going to shoot into the door."

He stepped back, raised his rifle and sent a three-shot burst into it.

He listened again. Still silent. The bullets did minimal damage to the heavy door. He wasn't sure but he thought he heard something like a whimper from inside.

"Come out or I'll shoot again."

Three more bullets dug into the door. No other sound.

"Tomas, see if there's something in the garage we can use to pry that open. I'm curious."

A little bit later Tomas returned carrying a crowbar.

"This outta do it." He wedged the bar into the seam of the door and pulled. It didn't budge. Both Tomas and Chris grabbed the bar and leaned back with all their weight. All they accomplished was to put a slight bend in the bar.

"Nuts!" Chris threw the bar on the ground. "Stay here and watch the door. If anybody comes out, grab 'em. I'm gonna report in to Miguel." He went back inside.

****

Chase worried about Char and Beau. Good thing they'd gotten to the safe room. He hoped the door would

192

hold against anything the attackers would throw at it. He guided the Mercury down the rain-slicked highway faster than he should, but he had to get home.

He also worried about his clothes. Stalking armed killers in dress shoes and civies was on top of the not-to-do list. His only hope was that the bad guys didn't know about the back path to the shack. If he could get inside, he'd have ample supplies to work with.

He rounded the bend in the road about a half mile from his destination. He cut the lights and slowly rolled to the path. So far, so good. No sign of intruders here. He pulled in and parked. He got out and listened. No unfamiliar sounds. He flicked the key fob to open the trunk.

Some time ago Chase had stuck a Glock with a belt holster and an extra magazine in the spare tire well as a precaution. Always be prepared was a good motto for him as well as the Boy Scouts. He pulled it out and checked the magazine. Fully loaded. He stuffed the extra mag in his pants pocket and as an after-thought he also grabbed a tire iron. Might come in handy, too.

He hooked the holster onto his belt and spotted an umbrella in the corner. He unfurled it and closed the trunk lid as quietly as possible. No human noises could be heard as he stood facing the mansion, trying once more to get an idea of where the attackers were. Still no clue.

Jogging down the path he concentrated on where he placed his feet. Mud oozed everywhere. The umbrella helped his vision but, in dress shoes, the going was treacherous. He almost fell twice before he reached the edge of path that gave him a view of his shack. He knelt and willed his night vision to kick in.

He rose up to approach the shack as three shots came from the direction of the mansion. Then he heard someone whispering in the grass off to his right. Another whisper came from a bit closer to the shack. Someone waited for him.

Chase put down the umbrella and lay down in the grass. He slithered toward the first whisperer. The rain and mud helped deaden his movements. He almost slid into a man crouching in the grass. The tire iron proved to be a valuable addition as he wacked the guy on the back of his head. The man fell on his side and went still.

A quick search yielded a rifle, ear buds, and ammo for the rifle. Chase put on the buds and checked the guy's boots. Nuts, too small. The man's weak pulse barely registered, but still there. He tied his hands and legs with the strings of his boot.

Chase shimmied back through the grass to the other side of the path. Three more shots rang out. He heard nothing further until a man yelled for someone to come out. They must have fired at the safe room door. *Good, it'd take a powerful round to penetrate that old door. Just stay inside Beau.*

Under the shack a man lit up a cigarette. He faced the mansion, so Chase darted for the grass area behind the shack. He made it with no sound giving him away.

So far, no instructions had come from the ear buds. *Everyone must be concentrating on trying to get into the safe room.*

Chase wiped rain from his eyes and searched the area under the shack. The glow of the cigarette came from the outermost stilt. A man squatted there holding a rifle. The man's hand was not on the trigger. Chase covered the distance quickly and tucked the tire iron under the man's chin and yanked hard. The man gagged and went limp. This time when Chase checked the pulse, he found none.

He ran up the stairs and into the shack. Changing into tactical pants and shirt, he donned a Kevlar vest and selected his favorite sniper rifle. Once he put on his boots, he felt whole and ready for anything. He tapped the ear buds.

"Can anyone join this party or is by invitation only?"

"What? Who is this?"

"Just call me a party crasher."

"You're messing with the wrong guy, Jack."

"I'm down here at the shack. Why don't you join me? We'll have an old-fashioned gunfight."

Chase wanted to get the attackers away from the main house, so Beau and Char were safe. He had a view of the house but could see no one. Thankfully the lights over the garage still blazed. Then he saw movement in the kitchen window. Just a glimpse of a man looking out.

The house was a good five hundred yards away. With little wind and an acceptable shot range he could probably take the guy out. But he didn't know how many others were lurking around wanting to shoot him.

Beau had said five or six. Two are now out of commission so besides the man in the house there was at least one maybe two left unaccounted for. He couldn't take a shot without making himself an instant target.

The ear buds activated.

"Tomas, report."

"Carlos, report."

"Joe, Report."

"I'm here. No one in sight."

"Tomas, Carlos, report."

Thanks so much for the info. So, five total. One guy whereabouts unknown. If the leader has any brains, which is still debatable, he'd have posted a guard at the gate to stop anyone else coming in.

The window curtain fluttered, and Chase spotted half a face peeking around it.

Chase tapped the ear buds.

"Your gang has had some vacancies recently. Tomas and Carlos are napping. One of them will need several Tylenol when he wakes up. Why don't you give up while you're still able to walk? I promise not to shoot if you toss out your weapons and come out on the porch.

"By the way, Joe. You need to give up, too. You no longer have back up. That noise you heard at the gate a minute ago was me. I let you live that time. I only give one chance."

"Fred what's going on? Where's Tomas and Carlos?"

"Shut up, Joe. He's pullin' your chain."

"I did hear something out here. This was supposed to be a piece of cake. It's a total screwup."

"Joe, throw down your gun and come back to the house. You won't die that way. Fred, you do the same and we'll all be the better for it."

Chase had to keep them concentrating on him.

****

Chris Martinez let loose of the kitchen curtain and slid away from the counter where he'd tried to see where Anderson was. This was turning into a fiasco. If he believed the man, two of his men were gone. Scratch

Tomas and Carlos.

A box on the wall held two sets of keys and Chris stuffed both in his pocket. One had to be for the Hummer. He hoped he and Alfredo would be able to find Anderson and take him out. He'd call Joe in so it would be three to one. Once finished they'd take the big car and escape. Now he had a plan.

He powered up his cell and called Miguel.

"We're here. We have Anderson surrounded and it's just a matter of time. Will be on silent for a while."

"Good. Let me know when it's done." Miguel hung up.

Chris hoped he had enough men left to do it. He lacked total confidence but being paid good money he had a job to do. He tapped his ear buds.

"Alfredo, hold your position. I'm coming to join you. Joe, you meet us there."

He crouched at the back door for a few seconds, then scooted down the steps. Alfredo was stationed at the corner of the garage and after a frightening run in the open drive, he dropped beside him.

"You good?" Chris asked.

"Good. Haven't seen anything yet."

"If he got Tomas and Carlos, he must be at the shack. When Joe gets here, we'll spread out and do a pincer move on the guy."

They waited and soon Joe appeared behind them coming from the back of the garage.

"I'm not so sure I really want to go through with this. If he did take out our guys, he has to be good. Carlos was an experienced fighter." Rain rolled steadily off the bill of Joe's baseball cap.

"Listen there's three of us. We can do this. We head

for the shack. Joe on the right flank and Alfredo on the left. I come from the middle and we all fire at the area underneath the shack. That's where he'll be. Best position for him. Got it?" Chris stared at each man.

"We'll have a lot of light behind us. Our silhouettes will be easy to spot." Joe pointed up to the powerful double beams lighting the entire parking area.

"That also means if he has it, he can't use night vision. And he'll be too busy dodging bullets to aim and fire." Chris held his hands palms up. "No problem. We keep to the tall grass until about a hundred yards from the shack. Then we separate and begin blasting. Okay?"

Alfredo nodded and Chris looked at Joe. Finally, he nodded. They crouched, ducked into the grass, and crawled toward the shack.

****

Chase slung his favorite rifle, a Chiappa M6 holding five .22 rimfire cartridges, onto his back as he climbed the stairs at the rear of the shack leading to the roof. He didn't need long-range capability tonight. And he had extra ammo just in case he needed it.

When Beau had the shack built, he'd added a small balcony area on top for terrific views of the bayou and property. A water-resistant two-foot-tall, metal guard rail surrounded the upper space.

He lay flat, resting his rifle on the rail as he settled behind it. Conversation on the ear buds gave him an idea of what they were planning. Then he watched as the man in the kitchen raced to the garage. He drew a bead on the guy and focused the telescopic lens. Not wanting to reveal his position yet, he didn't fire. He wanted all three to be where he could spot them with no trouble.

Chase remembered the many times he and Lily

enjoyed this view. The bayou was ever changing and full of wildlife. She loved it when a racoon or a deer ventured onto the grounds, squealing like a kid in sheer joy.

It had also been therapeutic during his recovery from his trauma. He usually felt close to Lily here. Though not so much now. She would've been adamant that there be no guns up there to mar the aura. Couldn't be helped.

The three men took cover in the grass and began crawling toward him. Looked like they were going for an all-out assault on the shack. This will be over soon. He zeroed in on each man, rehearsing the rifle swinging from one to the next. A night light under the shack had a button on the balcony that would activate it.

They crawled until they stopped about a hundred yards away. They'd make their move now. He flipped the light switch and light flooded the underside of the shack. He sighted on his first target. Slowing his breathing, he took in one long breath. One man ran to the left, and another to the right. The three fired simultaneously, spraying the bottom of the shack. The noise was deafening. The light took several hits and went out.

Birds exploded from the tree canopy, as three bullets left Chase's rifle. The men on each side fell first. The man in the middle did not suffer a killing shot. Instead, Chase had aimed for the man's knee. He knew personally how much pain that would cause.

The man screamed and dropped his rifle. The other men no longer able to scream didn't move. Silence returned to the bayou, except for the moans of the remaining attacker. Chase climbed down and approached. Kicking the man's weapon away, he knelt beside him.

"Hurts, don't it? I gave you a chance to get out of this with no harm. You disregarded that offer. Now you have one more chance to live. Give me the man's name who sent you after me, and where I can find him. I won't kill you. You'll need a good surgeon to fix your leg, but the state will pay for it."

Not long before the sirens of the police arrived, he had what he needed. A name and location. And he'd only had to tap the man's injured knee once.

Seven officers dressed in full tactical gear filed down the drive toward Chase. He placed his rifle on the ground in full view and raised his hands over his head.

"I live here. I have a knife and pistol on my belt." Chase stood next to the wounded attacker.

"Remove them carefully and lay them on the ground. Then step back three steps and turn around keeping your hands up."

He did so and one of the men came up and grabbed his hand and twisted it behind him. The men searched him, cuffed him, and ushered him to the porch. They said he wasn't under arrest but for everyone's safety handcuffs were required.

They also handcuffed the man moaning in the grass. EMTs were on their way. One deputy stayed with the man.

Chase sat uncomfortably in one of the deck chairs, hands cuffed behind him, as two uniforms unfurled crime scene tape around the house and shack and police investigators arrived to tag evidence. He'd called Beau and Char while waiting for the cops to show up, telling them to sit tight till the police wrapped up the scene. He assured them he was fine, and this would be over soon.

He didn't want them to see the carnage.

An ambulance arrived at the gate and two EMTs jogged down the driveway lugging heavy gear. They attended to the gunshot victim.

Finally, in what seemed like hours but was only minutes, Sheriff Tony Bernardo, hat in hand, walked up the stairs and stood next to him. He uncuffed Chase and sat.

"A fine mess you made here." He smiled and raked his hand through his short brown hair.

"Had a little cleanup to take care of."

"Let me get this straight. Five fully armed guys attacked this place, and you took them all out? Alone?"

"I guess that sums it up."

"I know you were Delta and all, but this is unreal."

"Actually Tony, they weren't competent. They did everything wrong, and I took advantage. Can I tell Beau and Char they can come out now?"

"Where are they?"

"I converted an old hurricane shelter into a safe room in the back of the house. They hid in there when these guys showed up."

"By all means. Glad to hear they're okay."

Chase made the call and soon Char, and Beau stormed the porch. Char threw her arms around Chase, hugging the breath out of him.

They sat and listened as Chase went over what had happened. Tony shook his head in disbelief. Beau and Char stared wide-eyed at him.

Tony stood and turned to leave. "Chase, right now I'm offering you the job of S.W.A.T. officer of Calcasieu Parish. I don't need any references, psychological profiles, or interviews. You want the job, come and talk.

I'm serious as a heart attack. I could use a man of your abilities. Think about it."

He left and they again were silent for a moment.

Beau pulled a cigar out of his pocket and a match. "Don't say anything, my dear. If ever a day I deserved a good smoke, this is the day. Chase, I don't know how to adequately say thank you. You saved our lives and we're eternally grateful."

"For once, I totally agree with you. Light up." Char turned from Beau to Chase and wiped a tear from her eye. "Thank you is such a meager response but it's all I have, Chase darling. Do you mind a hug instead?"

"Not at all." He stood and she again hugged him.

"Now, all these folks here investigating are gonna need some coffee and sandwiches. I better get started. Lettie will be here in a few minutes, and we got work to do." Char hustled off to the kitchen.

****

Lettie arrived a half hour later and jumped in to help Char with her preparations. Chase and Beau unwound in the dining room with some of Beau's best bourbon. Of course, the cigar was out and properly disposed of.

A steady stream of officers and police took advantage of the quick feast they had whipped up. Lettie came and motioned to Chase. They retreated to the huge library and sat in overstuffed leather chairs.

"You don't know how relieved I was when they said it was over and everyone was safe. I swear those minutes not knowin' what was goin' on were each an hour long at least. Char told me what you did. God bless you for keepin' them safe and tacklin' those men by yourself."

"Knowing they were in the safe room, and you were with the police gave me a peace of mind that helped keep me focused. Hey, you want a sandwich and some coffee? You know Char. We could feed an army."

"Don't know about you but I'm starved. Didn't get to finish my burger tonight."

"I'll only say yes if you promise me two things."

"Oh, now there's stipulations. Don't know if I like those." She smiled.

"Okay. One I get to help you fix our sandwiches so it's not anyone serving the other. We do it together."

"Guess I can live with that one. What's number two?"

"That we make another appointment," He held up his hands, palms out. "Not a date mind you, to finish that burger and get to our movie." He grinned.

"Well, excuse me. If we can't call it a date, then I may not be agreeable. After all this is almost our second appointment." She made air quotes around appointment and laughed.

Chapter 41

The Thibodeaux family plot tucked in the back corner of the Orange Grove Cemetery seemed peaceful. No paved roads circled the old portion of the grounds. Two dirt paths separated by a grass median led to Lily's grave. The branches of a huge camphor tree laced with moss hung low over the path as the car wobbled underneath.

This morning the sun's rays gently licked the stone marker. Chase got out of the Mercury and picked up the yellow rose bouquet. Lettie had driven him here early in his move to Louisiana, once he'd recovered from his three-month drinking bout. For only the second time since his relocation he approached and read the lettering. Lily Marie Thibodeaux Anderson.

He knelt and placed the roses in the empty holder next to the stone. He hesitated and then touched her name. Tears rolled down his face. He knew she wasn't really there. She had to be in heaven. But here, he at least wanted to try to connect with her.

Chase believed in God and heaven but was less than enthusiastic about a physical church and the many plastic Christians who professed their beliefs until they left the building. But if ever anyone deserved heaven, Lily did.

He rose, slowly turned and faced the sun, breathing in the flower smells and trying to embrace the sunlight. Old Louisiana cemeteries oozed peace and tranquility in the daytime. He turned back and knelt again, placing his hand on the stone.

"Hello, my love. Brought your favorite flowers. It's beautiful here today." He took a shuttered breath. "I just wanted to say I'm sorry. I know you're disappointed in me for what I've done. And you're going to be even more disappointed in what I'm about to do.

"This man in Chicago is the devil himself. He attacked our family and I have no doubt he'll not rest until he finally hurts one of us. I won't let that happen. I want you to rest easy, Darling. This is all on me. I won't rest until this is over.

"I know your God is forgiving. You said that a lot. I don't deserve forgiveness from him, but I'd be satisfied if you could see your way to forgive me." He touched the lettering once more. "I'll always love you. Goodbye."

He stood and walked back to the car. He was ready to finish what someone else started. He headed to Chicago.

Epilogue

Chicago, Illinois

Miguel whistled as he stashed several packages of fentanyl into his safe from the previous night's delivery. The warehouse he used as his office and holding area for his drugs and money was empty of all but three of his men. His most trusted lieutenants, Estaban and Ronaldo, stood on either side of the double door just inside the entrance. Rifles at the ready. Four cars in various levels of repair gleamed in the overhead lights.

Only Shonte Williams worked with Miguel to stack the drugs safely inside. Miguel closed the heavy door with a loud clank and set the code on the digital lock. His pride and joy, that vault. Seven feet tall and specially made for a bank in New Jersey.

Miguel had intercepted that shipment and installed the vault in his office. It occupied half the office space and had to have a reinforced floor added. State-of-the-art protection for his stash. He patted the safe door and turned to go. Thoughts of his nephew Jerman jolted him. He was like a son to Miguel.

Three wives had failed to give him children and Miquel had groomed Jerman to take over his empire. Now, a dashed hope. In the week since Jerman's death, Miguel had planned a final assault on that Anderson creep. The last attempt had cost him his nephew and a hundred million dollars' worth of pills.

Miguel sat down in the leather chair behind his desk and picked up a pen. He made some notes on a file in front of him and shoved it into an envelope to give to his office girl. He stood to call Shonte to get his car when he heard a noise. Like a puff, then another.

The two men at the door crumpled to the ground each with a bullet in the head. Shonte ducked down lying flat on the floor just inside the office, swinging his rifle back and forth trying to figure out where the muffled shots had come from. Then the warehouse lights flicked off.

"What's happening, Shonte?" Miguel screamed.

"Somebody got Esteban and Ronaldo. Can't see him."

Miguel yanked open the desk drawer and rummaged for his .357.

"Be a good idea to toss your weapons out. I can take you out easy from here. Quickly now." A voice echoed in the empty warehouse.

"Can you see him yet?" Miguel squinted against the darkness of the warehouse. He fumbled his way around the desk. The only remaining light was from the moon shining through the four upper windows.

"I'm not going to wait much longer. Throw out your guns. Now!"

Shonte whispered to Miguel. "He must be around the main control for the lights. I'll get him." He took aim and sprayed a full magazine into the walls around the power box. The box erupted in a splash of energy. He ejected the empty and reloaded. Silence. A heavy electrical burn smell wafted through the space.

"Maybe you got him." Miguel spit the words out.

"Nope. You missed. No more chances," the voice replied.

There was another puff of sound. Shonte grunted and fell silent.

"Shonte! Shonte? Who are you?" Miguel was seething now. He desperately wanted to see something to shoot at. Everything was black.

"I'm your worst nightmare, Miguel."

Miguel thought the voice came from the right, He fired three shots in that direction. Two of them clanked off a new BMW. He crawled toward the door.

"Not even close. Try again. I'm over here."

Definitely coming from the left now. He fired again. Nothing. Then he realized something terrifying. He'd fired three times but only two bullets left his gun. He'd forgotten to check his load and now he was out of ammo. He pounded the floor.

"Mister, I give up. Please don't shoot. Look I'm throwing my gun out." He tossed the empty pistol out the door. He unsnapped the fastener on the knife at his waist. He still had a weapon.

"Come out of the office, slowly with hands up."

Miguel got to his feet and moved to the door. He raised his hands and waited, wondering if the man would shoot him. No matter. He couldn't do anything unless he could get close to the guy. He wanted to press the point of his knife into that man's chest and twist. He wanted to, so bad.

****

Chase Anderson dressed in camouflaged shirt and pants and Army boots, walked up the aisle between a BMW and a Lexus. He stopped about five feet from Miguel with his rifle pointed down, but little movement would bring it on target.

"Do you know who I am?"

"You are somebody who is gonna pay for this."

"Looks to me like you're not in the best position to threaten anyone. My name is Chase Anderson. Do you recognize that name?"

"You…you killed my nephew. You have cost me much. I do not forget this."

"I had hoped we could put this whole episode behind us. Don't think that's possible. The crew you sent to kill me are all dead or in jail. Those guys weren't very good."

So that's why I haven't heard from Fred. "Can I put my hands down?"

Chase knew that wasn't a good idea, but he didn't want to kill in cold blood.

"Go ahead, put 'em down."

Miguel let his hands fall and drew his knife from its sheath at his side, swinging at Anderson. He tried to stab him bringing the knife down into his chest. Wrong move. Chase lifted his rifle up in a hard block. He felt the break of the bone in Miguel's forearm.

Miguel cried out and dropped the knife. He grabbed Chase's rifle by the barrel with his good hand and tried to wrestle it away. Chase brought the barrel straight up to break the grip. Then he stabbed the barrel into Miguel's chest, pulling the trigger.

The man looked down at his chest and sagged to the floor. Chase stood over Miguel and stared at the man who had attacked his family. Miguel struggled to speak. His mouth moved, but no sound escaped his lips. He choked and died.

Chase walked out of the warehouse to his rental car. He felt nothing as he dialed 911 on his burner phone. No remorse over Miguel, his nephew, the Washburns, or any of the others. No more than the enemies he'd encountered while in the military. Just a bunch of bad guys to be dealt with.

Finally, he was done with his wars. The ones overseas and the ones he'd fought here at home. Time to put his weapons away and return to the Bayou.

To his family.

A word about the author...

I have always written. Mostly short stories until I "retired" in 2002. Then I had three mysteries in trade paperback and eBook published by Wings ePress, Inc. My fourth book Smudge is available from Wild Rose Press.

I'm active in over 20 yahoo groups about writing and I own and moderate the Publishing and Promoting group with over 1000 authors and publishers worldwide providing a free source of tips and information pertaining to writing.

I taught an online three-week course titled How to Add Suspense to Your Killer Novel for Savvy Authors in 2010 and in 2014.

http://jdwebb.com

Thank you for purchasing
this publication of The Wild Rose Press, Inc.

For questions or more information
contact us at
info@thewildrosepress.com.

The Wild Rose Press, Inc.
www.thewildrosepress.com